FAST HOLIDAY

FAST LOVE SERIES
BOOK 2

KERRY LOCKHART

KEEN JEAN BOOKS LLC

Copyright © 2024 by Kerry Lockhart

ISBN: 979-8-9885404-2-7 (Fast Holiday ebook)

ISBN: 979-8-9885404-3-4 (Fast Holiday paperback)

Excerpt from *Fast Love* copyright © 2023 by Kerry Lockhart

ISBN: 979-8-9885404-1-0 (Fast Love paperback)

ISBN: 979-8-9885404-0-3 (Fast Love ebook)

Cover art by Steve Buccellato

Edited by The Authors' Assistant

For my best friend, Chris F.

CHAPTER 1

Sandy glanced over at Moonshine, his fuzzy-faced companion. The canine stood in the Prius's passenger seat, smushing her nose against the window. Sandy sighed at the vacant, snow-covered main street of Mayfield. The small town consisted of a two-lane downtown that was of the blink-and-you'll-miss-it variety. "What kind of man am I going to find in the sticks to keep me warm through the holidays? The answer is none. Zip. Zero. Nada. There won't be any bear bars out here unless they're of the wild animal kind—stuffed and mounted to a wall."

Moonshine tilted her head at him.

He checked the time on his phone. Noticing it was a couple of minutes past 8 a.m., he buttoned up his peacoat. "Don't look at me like that. I could be in a relationship if I wanted to, but who wants to be smothered all the time? Relationships are suffocating—my mom and step pops are a prime example. Why am I talking to you? I'm turning into Julia," he scoffed.

Moonshine barked as if in agreement.

With a last peek in the rearview mirror, he adjusted his ebony bangs to ensure they stayed out of his eyes. He turned his round face to the left and then the right, ensuring he hadn't left any candy cane residue on his face.

Sandy peered up at the historic three-story Italianate building. The name etched on the front window indicated that McCormick's General Store, circa 1982, had locations in both Mayfield, IL and Madison, WI. He had a feeling he'd be the only Korean-American in a several-hundred-mile radius. He sat up straight. *It's okay. You got this.* Sandy secured his red earmuffs over his head and tucked his red scarf tighter. He climbed out of the car and went around to the passenger door to gather Moonshine. "Okay, here's the deal. You have to be extra good. I need this gig to get me through the holidays. It's the only job left that has decent pay. My new job doesn't happen until after the new year, so, if you break it, you buy it. Understand me?"

She looked back at him with one ear lifted in disdain.

"Don't you dare pretend not to hear me." Sandy escorted Moonshine to the store's front door. The open sign was lit, but the doors didn't budge. He knocked once and then a few more times until a head of wavy reddish-brown hair weaved through the store, navigating toward Sandy. Whoa, a man the size of a lumberjack soon flipped open the front door locks. His flannel-clad arm held the door for Sandy and Moonshine.

"We don't allow dogs in the store," the lumberjack said

with his legs spread and hands on his hips. The stance would've been slightly intimidating if not for the hint of kindness around his mouth.

"I'm not a customer. I'm Sandy Holiday. I'm here for the interview." He removed his earmuffs as he stomped snow off his dress shoes, leaving wet clumps around him on the welcome rug.

The bearded woodsman gave him a quizzical once over. "It's already 8 a.m.?" He glanced at his FitBit and shook his head. A look of frustration stretched across his features before he returned his gaze to Sandy. "Your last name is Holiday?"

"Is there a problem with that?" Sandy tilted his head to the side, playfully curious about the Brawny Paper Towel guy. *He's so not my type. But, damn, I'd buy his paper towels.*

"It's—Are you pulling my leg? That's really your name? This morning is—Who are you?" The frown on the man's face deepened.

We're off to a catastrophic start. Shit. Do something. "I'm here for the Santa's Helper job. I know bringing a dog to an interview is unorthodox, but I'm dog sitting for a friend and with this weather and the long-ass drive from Chicago I couldn't abandon her. But Moonshine's not a normal dog. Okay, so she's a dog. Yes. But she's chill AF."

Moonshine let out a jubilant woof as if to prove Sandy's point.

"I'm Patrick McCormick, store manager." His lips turned down as he studied the dog. "The start to this day has been unusual."

"Oh, this might fill you with cheer . . . " Sandy ran to a

nearby display of reindeer antler headbands. He grabbed a pair and placed them on Moonshine's head. "Ta-dah! Instant reindeer. And she's great with kids, adults, and, ah, I dunno . . . fish? She could totally be the store mascot for the holiday season. That'd break TikTok."

The response from Patrick wasn't as thrilled as Sandy would've liked; in fact, the guy seemed like someone had rammed coal up his nose. Sandy didn't know what to think of this handsome, yet detached, guy.

"Follow me." As Patrick climbed the stairs, Sandy couldn't help but notice the thick jean-clad thighs in front of him and the very tight butt. However, Sandy didn't have much time to stare. Patrick was so quick on his feet that Sandy and Moonshine had to jog to keep up.

With sluggish fingers, Sandy struggled to untie his scarf and unbutton his peacoat. By the time they arrived at Patrick's third floor office sweat poured down his back and his lungs heaved like an Alaskan husky after running the Iditarod.

Patrick pointed to hooks by the door. "Feel free to hang your stuff." He rounded his desk and wiggled his mouse. His eyes scanned the screen. A deep crease formed between Patrick's eyebrows.

Uncertain of his impression on the other man, he felt a flutter of panic in his stomach as he hung his things. *Is it me or is this guy super uptight? Maybe I could lighten the mood?* "You don't have chairs? Or a chair?" He unhooked Moonshine's leash, placing that on a hook, too.

Patrick concentrated on navigating, his features down-turned as if annoyed. "They take up space."

"Yeah, and it's so jam-packed with stuff in here." Sandy took in the spartan room. The shelves, organized with binders dating back a decade, were neatly labeled accordingly for taxes, employees, and inventory. The office contained nothing else except Patrick's computer and standing desk.

"This idiotic platform isn't bringing up your information." Patrick slammed his mouse down. The plastic cracked, startling Sandy.

Oof, this guy is tough. Where's a nutcracker when I need one? Be charming but not too enthusiastic. Sandy swayed back on his heels as he stood in the middle of the room with Moonshine. "Hey, I'm right here. Why don't you fire away with any questions you have?"

"Do you drink?"

"Well, I—What?"   Sandy stumbled, confused by the random inquiry.

Patrick ran a thick hand through his hair. "I fired a drunk photographer this morning, so I'm off my game."

"You're kidding me? That's what I am. A photographer." A glimmer of hope ran through Sandy. He took the liberty of rounding Patrick's desk. *Firing an employee explains why he's so grumpy.* "Do you mind?"

Patrick's brows scrunched together like there was a protest in the making, but Sandy didn't wait. He took control of Patrick's keyboard and mouse, clicking to display his website. "My portfolio."

The sound of Patrick inhaling practically echoed around the room. The scowl lifted from his face. "Did you eat a candy cane recently?"

The heat of embarrassment hit Sandy's cheeks. He couldn't resist those mini candy canes during the holidays. And the drive out to Mayfield had lasted forever. The long trek combined with nervous tension had him scarfing half the bag before he arrived.

"No wonder you have so much energy. You'll regret that choice once the sugar wears off," Patrick said all that in an accusatory tone before scrolling the photos. "These are impressive."

Under Patrick's desk, Moonshine's tail swished back and forth like a metronome, hitting Patrick's Red Wing work boot.

"You two should take your show on the road." Patrick raised a brow at the dog.

Is he lightening up? Keep doing whatever you're doing, Moonshine. "Oh, she's not my dog. She's my best friend's girlfriend's mutt."

Moonshine growled as if insulted by the derogatory remark.

"Sorry," Sandy said to Moonshine. "She's not a mutt. She's half bearded collie and half human." Sandy met Patrick's startling green eyes. *Wow. He's like an Irish lumberjack. So not my type, but that color's more beautiful than a Christmas tree.* Patrick's woodsy scent lingered between them. They were standing closer than Sandy realized.

Patrick cleared his throat. "Would you mind going to the other side of the desk?"

The warmth of Patrick's breath hit Sandy, throwing him off balance. *Damn, is this the candy cane high? Must be the candy canes.* He nodded and then gave a brisk whistle for Moonshine.

"It'll be full-time. Provided your background check clears —should have that any minute now. Would you be able to start today?"

"Yes, and the pay is $40 an hour?"

Patrick's eyes bulged. "No, $17."

Sandy deflated and stuck his hands in his pants pockets. There was no way he could take the job for that kind of money. The commute wouldn't be worth it. He'd have to find something else.

With folded arms, Patrick glanced at his computer and then at Sandy. "Listen, if you can do the photographer's job along with playing Santa's Helper, then I can swing forty. Deal?"

Sandy stepped forward, holding out his hand. "Done."

Moonshine let out a couple happy barks as they shook.

"What about a live reindeer?" Sandy wiggled his eyebrows in Moonshine's direction.

A sign escaped from Patrick as he ran a hand through his hair, which Sandy clocked as some kind of stress-induced reflex. "I'm not insured for dog bites, so I'll need you to sign a waiver that she's had her shots. It's all on you if she takes a chunk out of someone."

"Fantastic!" Sandy pulled a biscuit out of his pocket for Moonshine. The dog sat, rolled over, and sat again. He tossed the treat into the air and Moonshine lept up and caught it.

Patrick shot him a curious glare. *This guy is so buttoned up. Does he even know how to relax? I'm making it my mission to remove the antlers lodged from his backside.*

"Let me show you the locker room and costume."

"Ooo, dress-up time." Sandy clapped. He turned and pointed at the dog. "Moonshine. Stay."

Moonshine spun around in a circle and laid down.

"I dunno if you had time to look at our products online," Patrick said, as he led the way. "We sell everything from clothing to sports equipment, outdoor goods, and toys. The holiday hours are different from our regular hours. I'll email you that information." Patrick pushed open the Staff Only door. "It's unisex with a shower, but no one ever uses that. Well, I do. Sometimes."

The corners of Sandy's mouth twitched. *No. No, dirty thoughts. Stop it right now. Do you hear me? No sudsy, steamy daydreams about your new boss. He's bland. Boring. And sweet Kelly Clarkson, he's the opposite of glowing.*

Twenty full-sized metal lockers painted the store colors, Kelly green and cream white, lined the walls. The room smelled like a pinecone. A Christmas tree stood in the corner with little handmade ornaments clinging to the branches.

Patrick nodded at the dangling decorations. "We had an ornament party."

A rolling rack stood at the back wall. Patrick unzipped one of the garment bags. A bright red, green, and white costume appeared. "This is the elf suit. We use the same ones every year. Don't worry, they're dry cleaned."

"No cooties then?"

"No." Patrick zipped up the bag. "On to tech and camera stuff."

Does this guy have a sense of humor, or has his flannel shirt suffocated it out of him? They headed out of the locker room and toward the stairs.

"No wonder you're so athletic. These stairs are insane."

"Ah, thanks." Patrick clutched a palm around the railing as if the compliment threw him off balance. "The elevators are too slow for me. I don't like waiting. Santa's workshop's located on the first floor." Patrick rounded the post at the end of the stairs, almost colliding with someone wearing an elf suit. "Perfect timing—you two are going to be working together. Sandy meet Chelsea. Pronouns are they/them."

Whew, someone to give me a break from this too serious jockstrap. Sandy shook hands with Chelsea. "He/him/his or Sandy the Elf, or I also respond to 'I've got candy.'"

Chelsea adjusted the elf hat, and a flicker of a smile appeared and disappeared on their face. They turned and headed to the Workshop.

There must be some kind of moody epidemic going on in this village. "They are extraordinarily chatty." Sandy wondered how he'd make it through the holidays if everyone was this congenial.

Patrick walked away as if expecting him to follow. "Don't take it personally. Chelsea doesn't do small talk. I think you two will work well together."

Sandy wasn't so certain. He jogged to keep up as they zigzagged through clothing racks and aisles until Patrick stopped with a hand stretched as if expecting to stop and admire Santa's Workshop.

Santa's throne and workshop were a child's dream. The cozy structure resembled a gingerbread house, filled with candy, toys, and video games. Fake snow fell from automated machines, and holiday music filled the air. Cookies, popcorn, and hot chocolate stations were interspersed with booths for kids to make ornaments and wrap gifts.

Patrick led Sandy to the inner sanctum, behind the curtains. "This is where Santa, the elves, and the magic happens." A tabletop was cluttered with a camera, a printer, headphones, and a ton of cables. "You'll print out the photos after the kids pose with Santa."

Sandy ran a hand down his tie, considering the equipment before him. He picked up the Canon and inspected it, before returning it to the table. "You're not serious, are you?"

Patrick's back went rigid at the question. "What's the problem? This is part of the tradition at the store. If you don't like it, then feel free to get the heck out of here."

Sandy placed a hand on Patrick's shoulder and then removed it immediately. The last thing he needed was for this guy to think he was hitting on him. "This camera is from the '90s. Possibly the 1890s." He let out a bubble of laughter to show he was mostly joking.

"We can't afford anything else. We print out the copies for our customers and they love it, so if you have a problem with this then maybe this isn't the job for you." Patrick gritted his teeth.

"Whoa, hang on. Not at all." He reached out to place a

hand on Patrick's forearm and stopped himself. "I'm a professional photographer. Let me bring in my own equipment. The camera, the lights . . . you won't have to print, which means you'll save money. I can email or text high-res images, and for the rare customer who wants a print I can create high-end quality images. You can charge more in those instances."

"You can do all that?" Patrick asked.

"Sure, and if they want anything matted, mounted, and framed, we'll figure out an invoicing and delivery plan. Or we could set up a page for them to purchase off your website —kind of like they do for marathon runners?"

Patrick's throat bobbed as if he were swallowing a ball of ice.

Sandy couldn't figure out if the silence from the other man was a good thing or a bad thing, but he pressed onward. "It'll cost them a lot more to frame. I'll need to receive a percentage for the time and be reimbursed for the materials."

"That could work," he said with marginal enthusiasm, but Sandy took the comment as a full-throated go ahead.

With a loud, "Woo-hoo!" he threw his arms into the air. "Let's do this. I have my travel camera with me, which will work for today, and then I can bring everything else from home this afternoon or tomorrow morning."

The deep crease between Patrick's eyes returned. "First, I need you to go with Chelsea. You can't wear your fancy clothes. Go to the second floor, get some jeans, a flannel, and we'll dig out some boots for you."

CHAPTER 2

I n front of a mirror in the locker room, Sandy scrutinized the flannel button-down and jeans. His best friend Julia peered at him from the iPhone he clutched like a lifeline. "Are you seeing this? I mean what the F kind of torture is this?"

Moonshine sneezed.

Julia yawned as the airport chaos loomed behind her. "Are there bells on those boots? I hear ringing."

He glared at the mirror, daring her to repeat the question. He turned to the left and then the right. No angle seemed to make this disaster work. "Obvi this guy hates me. I came in here wearing silk and he's in flannel. I don't blame him." Sandy put a boot on the bench to tie the shoestrings.

"Flannel is nice," Julia responded with her typical snark.

He scrunched his nose. "He had on blue and white flannel of the variety that men in retirement homes favor. With boots and jeans. Like this hot mess! This guy is like the epitome of a Midwestern dude. I wouldn't be surprised if his house was decorated with a bunch of dead animal heads. What am I supposed to do with that?"

Julia propped her feet on her carry-on bag and shrugged.

"We don't agree on anything. It's a horrible combination —like eggnog and peppermint schnapps. And everything that comes out of my mouth seems to offend him or turn him into an angry elf. A giant angry elf. With these amazing biceps." He held up his hands to demonstrate the size.

"So, not your type and not rip roaring handsome?"

He pursed his lips. "He is—in an annoying way. He looks like a lumberjack leprechaun. I will bet you a zillion dollars he likes the outdoors, and I know he likes kids, which is stupid. And wait, why are we talking about my boss? We should be talking about the fact that I got a job and your girlfriend's dog got a gig, too. We gonna get paid!" Sandy said to Moonshine as he wiggled around in a circle. Excited by the dancing, Moonshine wagged her tail too.

A knock came from the locker room door.

"Come in," Sandy shouted.

Chelsea stuck their head around the door.

Sandy waved to Julia. "I gotta go. Hope your flight isn't delayed much longer. Happy travels!" He disconnected and took his jacket from Chelsea at the door. "What about Moonshine?"

They looked at the dog. "Patrick's office. He could use a friend."

Sandy smiled at the ribbing. *Maybe one person here has a sense of humor.*

Together, they dropped Moonshine off in the office. Chelsea pulled a towel from a closet and laid it on the floor.

"Water bowl?" Sandy asked.

Chelsea made a *hmm* sound, then popped open the door to a mini-fridge in the corner and pulled out a Tupperware of what looked like stew.

"I hope that's not Patrick's lunch."

"It smells like it's gone off. We're saving his life." They filled the square container with water in Patrick's bathroom. They set it next to Moonshine's makeshift bed and patted her on the head.

"I kinda can't believe how chill everyone is about having a dog here. This wouldn't fly in Chicago." He wrapped his scarf around his neck and tucked it into his jacket, preparing for the cold.

Chelsea zipped their jacket and pulled on a pair of deer-skin gloves as they led them out of the office. "We're not the city."

"Fantastic." He picked up his pace to keep up with them. *Does everyone in this town move this fast?*

Outside, Sandy put on his earmuffs. The wind had picked up.

Chelsea pulled a key fob from their pocket, aiming it at the blue Silverado parked in front of the store.

"Where are we headed?" Sandy slid into the passenger seat, closing the door and securing his seat belt.

They started the truck and gave a nod to the end of Main

Street. "Today is the pre-holiday celebration at the store." Chelsea drove and turned down a side street, leading them to the rear of a café. They turned the vehicle around and backed into a spot by the exit.

"Come on," Chelsea said as they climbed out the door.

Together they folded up the truck bed cover. Chelsea dropped the gate before they entered the establishment.

"This is Viv's Café." They pointed at a large, empty coffee urn sitting on a rectangular table filled with assorted supplies and baked goods. "All of these donations will go to the store."

Sandy nodded as he picked up the urn and a canister of ground coffee. "What goes down at this thing? Besides people going to town on these goodies?"

Chelsea filled their hands with packaged holiday linens. "You're a curious person."

Sandy blurted out a laugh. "And you don't like talking. I'm going to try and change that."

Their stoic face didn't flinch.

With arms full of napkins and cups, Sandy leaned against the door propping it open for Chelsea. "What's the deal with Patrick? Is he always wound tighter than a Christmas clock?"

They nodded and a sigh slipped out as they loaded the truck. "He's under a lot of stress. The store is in transition."

"In trouble?"

They grunted instead of answering, which Sandy took to mean yes.

"Between you and me, the website could use a facelift. It looks like it was created a hundred years ago, and the color scheme is completely different from what I saw at the store. Plus, not to be a total nag, but it reeks of 2010." That earned him a barely audible laugh from Chelsea as they made their way back inside the cafe.

Chelsea loaded trays of pastries into Sandy's arms.

He concentrated on holding the baked goods and not dropping them. "I used to handle the social media for a bookstore, and, sure, it's a different beast, but it's still retail, so do you think Patrick would be open to a discussion about it?"

They followed behind Sandy as they walked. "Maybe . . . Don't dump all over him."

"Oh, no, no that's not—shit. Sometimes my mouth runs away from me. I'll try to be less of an asshat when I chat with him." *Ugh, I really gotta get a hold of myself. Do not insult Patrick, and don't inadvertently touch him. Or ogle his ass.* He blew his bangs off his forehead.

After they returned to the store, Sandy placed his camera bag behind the curtain. He and Chelsea set up the tables and laid out the baked goods next to the cider and coffee inside of Santa's Workshop. Sandy took his camera out, firing off several sample shots of the set-up. He managed to get a few of Chelsea and Patrick. Personalizing it with people instead of only products would do wonders for the website.

"When does the store open?" Sandy cracked the cellophane on a couple of boxes of candy canes and dumped them into a bowl.

Patrick placed his hands on his hips. That pinched look on his face returned. "We've been open since eight this morning."

So much for not insulting him and his family business. "I guess people are waiting for the celebration. That makes perfect sense." Ugh, he'd epically failed to smooth over this conversation. In his defense, he hadn't seen one customer since he'd arrived, and he hadn't seen any since the set up. It was after ten. A flicker of worry grew in his stomach. *How will this place survive through the holiday season?* Sandy stepped up to Patrick. "I want to offer my services to help with social media and marketing."

"Did Chelsea say something to you?"

"Not at all. It's . . . " Sandy spread a hand out as if to say "look around" here. "Maybe things could use a boost?"

"It'll pick up. The community always comes through for the celebration. Speaking of, you need to get upstairs and change. Also, I have some songs that we sing printed out for you on my desk. Will the dog be okay in a crowd?"

Sandy tossed empty candy boxes into a recycle bin. "Yes, sir, boss man. And, yup, she'll be amazing. Moonshine's a people person." *Boss man? Yeesh, who am I?* He tucked his camera bag away and then started toward the stairs.

He stopped by Patrick's office. Moonshine trotted to him, and he gave the furry animal a pat on the head and a few scratches behind her ears. "Please tell me you didn't pee on anything."

Moonshine gave a woof, which kind of sounded like she was offended by the suggestion.

Sandy snatched the music off the desk. "You need to visit the outdoors before this shindig. Come on."

Inside the locker room, Sandy changed into the elf

costume and snapped a few selfies. *Yeah, I can pull off anything, even bells on my shoes and a floppy felt hat.* Sandy attached Moonshine's leash and led her to the back exit. Walking in the ridiculous jingling elf shoes slowed the process. He opened the back door and let Moonshine run out on her own, seeing as he didn't want to risk getting snow or anything else on them.

Just as Chelsea came down the hall, Moonshine ran back inside. Sandy attached the leash and her antlers. "Okay, we're ready."

They nodded. "When Santa comes down the stairs, we'll start singing."

Sandy gave a thumbs up as excitement ran through him. This was ridiculously fun. He followed behind Chelsea as they walked to the workshop. Surprisingly, the store had filled up with dozens of adults and children.

Chelsea turned to him. "Okay, now."

As Santa gave out a jolly laugh from the first stairstep, the usually monosyllabic Chelsea burst out the opening lines to "All Alone on Christmas." A huge smile spread across Sandy's mouth, and he started to sing, too. And then everyone joined in as Santa ho-ho-hoed his way through the crowd.

When Sandy belted out the lyrics to the next song all he could think was that Patrick had been right. The community sure did show up for McCormick's. *But where was Patrick?* Surely, he wouldn't be working on the books while this celebration was happening. Sandy glanced around the faces in the crowd, but he wasn't anywhere to be found.

Santa led the elves and the dog to his chair. As the song died down, Sandy ordered Moonshine to sit next to Santa's chair on the stage. Then he popped behind the curtain and grabbed his camera. Patrick didn't say anything about shooting the event, but he'd be foolish not to take the opportunity to snap some photos.

"Ho! Ho! Ho!" Santa's voice boomed. "Welcome one and all to McCormick's Holiday Celebration. I flew into town and will be here all month to celebrate with my favorite friends and family in Mayfield. Please help yourselves to the pastries and refreshments."

A small girl wrapped up in a jacket as if she were a character from South Park tugged on Sandy's costume. "I like your dog deer. Can I pet them?"

Sandy bent down to the kid. "Sure. Like this." He held his hand up to Moonshine's nose, showing her how to introduce herself to the dog.

The girl followed his instructions. "Don't dogs get cold in the North Pole?"

"She has fur and sweaters. But she works mostly inside instead of out."

"Like baking cookies?"

"More like consuming them if you don't keep an eye on her."

"You're funny." The girl's mother took her hand and led them to the photo line.

Wow. Kids are so easy. I'm amazing at this job. Sandy locked his camera down into the tripod and adjusted the focus. Then he stepped up to Santa. "Hi, ah, Santa, I need to make some adjustments to your beard and jacket. You good with that?"

"Do what you need to do." Santa winked at him.

"Don't mind if I do." Sandy pulled the ends of the wig out of the suit, laying it down, and straightened the beard, blocking Santa from the children's eyes. "There we go, that's much better. You look very handsome. I bet the missus loves this beard."

"Ho, ho, ho, I'm not married. Are you?" A blush rose in Santa's cheeks.

Is Santa flirting with me? RuPaul help me, I do love a beer belly. "Nope, this elf is as free as a reindeer. We'll have to chat before you fly off on your sleigh."

"My sleigh has room for one more."

"Oh, Santa, you're a bad boy." Admittedly, he shouldn't be bantering with a guy whose face and body he'd yet to see. But so far his winter had been awfully cold and lonely, and rolling around with Santa had moved to the top of his must-have list, so he wasn't about to stop these shenanigans. "I might have to come sit on your lap a little later and tell you what I really want for Christmas." Sandy chuckled as he returned to his camera.

CHAPTER 3

Patrick adjusted the glasses on the tip of his nose as he waited for the next child to climb the stairs with Chelsea to share their Christmas list. Patrick loved playing Santa. Granted, he couldn't figure out what got into him when he started flirting with Sandy. *He's an employee for crying out loud, and you just met the guy. No more out of character flirting.*

Sure, Sandy looked cute in the elf costume, and he was this giant ball of fun sunshine, but five minutes ago he was unhappy with the man for offering up his marketing knowledge to help save the store. He'd have to stop being so sullen and accept the fact that Sandy's good intentions were just that —generosity of spirit. The last time he trusted someone, outside of Chelsea, that had backfired on him and his family.

Chelsea ushered six-year-old twins to his chair. "Santa,

this is Greg and Mindy. Okay, you two ready to tell Santa what you'd like this year?"

"Hello, have you two been good this year?" Patrick asked his standard Santa question.

The bashful twins crawled into the chair beside him and quietly shared their gift wishes. They took extra time, but Patrick didn't mind. Their single mom worked hard to provide for them. He made a note to guarantee they got what they needed through the store's toy drive program.

A couple of hours later, Sandy flagged Chelsea over, and they moved to the steps by Patrick. "I need to swap out the battery on the camera before we continue with the next round."

"Perfect timing." Patrick winked at Sandy. "We're ready for more carols." As he stood, Sandy scooted around to the curtained area. "We're going to take a musical interlude with my right-hand elf."

Chelsea stepped up to the microphone.

Patrick and the entire store turned quiet as they sang an acoustic version of "Happy Christmas."

Across the stage, Patrick caught Sandy as he stuck his head out from behind the curtain with a look of shock. Chelsea's beautiful voice. Patrick met Sandy's gaze. There was interest and curiosity in that look. *Is it because I'm Santa, or does Sandy know it's me beneath the costume?* He shook his head, almost missing his cue to join in the song, and raised his arms to get the crowd to sing along. At the end everyone clapped and cheered. A few folks even had tears in their eyes.

A surge of joy ran up his spine. This was what it was all

about—bringing the community together and sharing a bit of happiness. Even the building landlord and his family had shown up today. And Patrick spotted purple-haired Viv from the café, her three sons, and a slew of grandkids. Thankfully, the writer/photographer attended from the weekly newspaper, *The Cardinal*, which would get the store some positive coverage. Patrick had spoken with his parents last night, and due to the icy conditions between Madison and Mayfield, they'd decided it would be best for them to travel after the roads were treated.

An hour later, the photo line had emptied. Sandy worked with a few families that wanted printouts right away, and Chelsea started a story time session for the kids. In his Santa persona, Patrick shook hands with the crowd and strolled toward the hot beverage station, for a cup of cider. Jim, the property landlord, stopped next to him.

"Hey, you got a minute?"

"Sure thing. Let's go up to my office." He led the way through the crowd and took them upstairs. Once inside, he closed the door and removed his beard, wig, hat, and glasses. "What can I do for you?"

Jim scratched his ear. "I really hate doing this—today of all days."

Patrick folded his arms across his chest, preparing himself for whatever news Jim needed to share.

The landlord pulled an envelope out of his jacket pocket and handed it to Patrick.

The bottom dropped out of Patrick's stomach as he scanned the contents. "You're evicting us?"

Jim stepped closer to the desk. "It's a ninety-day notice. If you can get the back rent paid by then, this can be torn up, but if not . . . it's nothing personal. I can't afford to let this slide any longer."

Patrick ran a hand through his hair. He knew he was late on the rent, but he hoped to get another loan at the bank. But they still hadn't given him an answer. His face burned with frustration and the thick padded costume became stifling. "What about a payment plan? Small payments to gradually get the store back on its feet."

"I don't have that kind of time. If the store can't make the monthly fees, then I need to try and get another business in here that can. Maybe if you call your dad he could . . . "

Patrick shook his head. That wasn't an option. "Thanks for coming out today and bringing your family. It means a lot even though . . . " Patrick held the notice up because he couldn't finish the sentence.

"Take care, Patrick." Jim turned and slipped out of the office.

As the door clicked shut, Patrick crumpled the paper in his hand. He wasn't a violent man, but damn if he didn't want to punch the living daylights out of something right now. Ten years of his life and this was all he had to show for it. Ten years of living in a small town, making some friends, and suffering through a few failed relationships. And now the worst part of it all was delivering the news to his mom and dad. He could imagine the devastation in his dad's eyes. One son had stolen from the family and the other ran a store into the ground.

Patrick needed to get out of this damned costume before he burst into flames. He stormed out of his office and headed into the locker room. He tossed his belt on a bench, then went for the jacket and shirt with the fake belly. He was so angry he slammed a door on one of the lockers. The action felt so good he repeated it . . . over and over and over again.

"Ah . . . hi." Sandy stood at the door, frozen in place—as if he was too afraid to move or breathe.

Patrick's face heated up and each painful breath scaled his lungs. And he probably looked like a deranged Santa, half-dressed and assaulting an inanimate object as if his life depended on it. But he didn't care. He had failed the store and his family, and his world was officially unraveling. "Do you need something?"

"You're Santa?" Sandy said in a voice full of wonder.

"What of it?" Patrick growled. The vein in his neck throbbed.

With hands held up in surrender, Sandy seemed to gingerly approach him. "We have one more kid who'd like a photo op with, well, you."

Patrick wiped a hand across his face. His palm came away damp with sweat. Not much of a shocker, really, seeing as the suit mixed with his temper had turned his body into a frigging furnace.

"I can tell him no. I'm great at denying children their dreams," Sandy snarked.

Too drained from his emotional outburst to care about anything anymore, Patrick shook his head. "Don't do that."

"Personally, I think you should go downstairs just as you

are." Sandy handed the shirt and belly over to him. "Are you alright?"

Patrick grunted. "Tell them I'll be right there."

Sandy gave a curt nod and disappeared out the door.

Fucking great. He's going to think I've got anger management issues. But I think I'm allowed to have them today of all days.

———

As Sandy came down the stairs, visions of Patrick's ripped torso danced through his head. *Holy shirtballs! I did not see those abs coming.* And the way Patrick's eyes turned an even darker, sexier shade of green when he was mad! Sandy waved a hand in front of his face when he remembered how hot angry Santa had looked. It made him wonder how naughty he'd have to be to get a fiery reaction from Santa.

"Is he coming down?" Chelsea met up with Sandy on the floor.

He nodded in a trance-like state. His brain had officially left the building.

"You look weird."

Sandy blinked himself back to reality. "I think something or someone pissed Patrick off. He was beating the living snot out of a door, and he looked like one of those cartoon bulls where the steam rolls out of their nose."

Their features scrunched up like they needed to solve a puzzle.

Santa walked up to the stage.

Sandy and Chelsea took their places. Sandy aimed and

shot photos of the last kid with Santa. Something about Patrick had changed. The teasing from before was gone, and his anger was back in full swing. Even with the final child, Sandy couldn't get Patrick to relax or smile like before. Dissatisfied with the photo, he called it quits, hoping that this really was the end of the day.

Sandy put a foot on one of the steps leading to Santa and Chelsea. "I'm going to start uploading the photos onto the laptop."

"Use my office," Patrick mumbled as he stood and marched away.

"Don't worry. There's a folding chair in his closet in the office."

"Lifesaver." Sandy shot them a smile and headed behind the curtain to pick up the rest of his things. He snagged Moonshine from the stage.

After a quick doggie break and a detour to get dog food from the car, they made themselves at home in Patrick's office. Moonshine flopped down on her makeshift bed and relaxed.

"That's exactly how I feel," Sandy said to the furry dog as he lowered the standing desk and retrieved the folding chair. As soon as he sat down, relief hit his legs. "Oh yeah, Daddy like." He tossed his hat onto the desk and flipped open the laptop. The next few hours of uploading the photos from his camera onto a site seemed to take forever. The next time he looked up at the clock he was shocked to learn it was after eight.

Chelsea stopped by the door to the office. They stood in

their regular clothes, shrugging into their jacket. "You're done for the day."

Sandy stretched and yawned. "Am I? Thank the bejesus cuz I am exhausted. Who knew being an elf is the most exhausting job on the face of the earth?"

Chelsea pulled a stocking cap out of their pocket. "Are you hungry?"

"I could eat a cow. Seriously, point one out and I'll tackle it and eat it caveman style."

The corners of Chelsea's mouth turned up. "Get changed and meet me outside."

Sandy flipped the laptop shut. In record time he changed. Somehow, he hadn't seen Patrick for the rest of the day, and even now his boss didn't check in with him. He grabbed Moonshine and his jacket and headed downstairs.

He found Chelsea outside. Snow fell, but thankfully the wind had died down completely. For an Illinois winter night, the windchill no longer cut through him like a knife.

"Wherever we go, they better like dogs."

Moonshine wagged her tail, approving that suggestion.

Chelsea tilted her head for the pair to follow them down the street.

All the other businesses on Main Street—Cathy's Cuts Salon, the T-Shirt Shack, The Cardinal—were closed for the night. The black-painted lamp posts lit up the sidewalks, and the holiday lights hung from wires above gave the town a cozy feel. The brisk walk went quickly as they traveled the six doors down from McCormick's.

Chelsea held the door open to Ace's High Bar for Sandy

and Moonshine. Sandy dusted the snow off his jacket. Moon-shine followed suit and shook herself.

Ace's small, square interior looked like it couldn't hold more than a hundred people comfortably. The reclaimed pine plank ceiling and walls gave the place the illusion of a cabin. Warm lighting and a corner fireplace provided an overall cozy atmosphere. Four high-topped tables stood against a wall near a karaoke. The place smelled clean, to Sandy's surprise, a mix of Pine-Sol and spirits.

Off the scowl of a burly man behind the bar, Sandy turned to Chelsea. "Are you sure it's okay for us to have Moonshine in here?"

A short auburn-haired woman wearing a knitted Santa's stocking cap bounced over to them and bent down to pet Moonshine. "Don't mind Randy. He loves dogs but is wary of strangers. Hi, Chels."

Chelsea nodded at the waitress as they unzipped their jacket and hung it on a rack near the front door.

"I don't blame him. Normally, I'm not a fan either." Sandy waved at the bartender just to prove he could be friendly.

The waitress stood. "Sit anywhere you like." She grabbed a couple of menus from the bar counter. "Flag me down when you're ready."

Sandy took the lead and beelined them to a table next to the stage. He removed his jacket and placed it on the back of his chair. Moonshine took the liberty of lying down on the edge of the stage. Sandy tilted his head at his preoccupied dinner companion. Chelsea seemed to have their gaze trained on the auburn-haired woman. "How do you know the waitress?"

"High school. Sam. Samantha. Gómez."

"As in the Addams Family?"

Chelsea made some sort of sound at the back of their throat.

Sandy laid a hand flat on the table. "Okay, you have to start using full sentences if we're going to hang out because I don't speak Morse code or whatever the hell kind of short-hand you're doin'."

Chelsea returned their attention back to Sandy with their head dipped down.

"So, you like Sam?"

Chelsea jerked their head up. Their cheeks turned pink. "We used to know one another."

A smug smile graced his lips. "Yeah, we're gonna need some dranks." He held a hand in the air to Sam, who hustled over with a couple of waters. "I need something strong because I had to deal with children all day long and a grumpy Santa."

Sam chuckled as if she could relate.

"And something extremely unhealthy to eat." Sandy scanned the menu. "This double burger thing. And your very best tap water for my canine friend."

Sam focused on Chelsea. "Your usual?"

Sandy could've been wrong, but Sam's voice seemed to take on a sultry tone when she spoke to the gentle giant.

"Thanks." Chelsea gulped down the water like they were in a desert.

Once Sam left, Sandy planted his elbows on the table to lean in for a confidential chat with Chelsea. "Did you two bang once upon a time? Cuz I'm getting serious lady/non-binary wood vibes between you two."

Chelsea clapped a hand over their mouth to keep water from shooting out. Chelsea took a moment to breathe. "Not ever. And you should talk. What was all that between you and Patrick today? I thought I was going to have to take the children to a safe space."

"Ah ha! They can speak!" Sandy was delighted that he finally got them to break out of their shell. "I had no idea that Patrick was Santa until I saw him shirtless in the locker room. And normally the extremely fit are not on my to-do list, but he is one fine piece of man morsel. Truth, I may have drooled on myself."

That earned him a genuine smile from Chelsea.

"Not that I'm interested in him. I'm not. I can just appreciate pretty things. Have you known him long?"

"I've known Patrick and his family forever. I worked for his dad when I was in high school. And then when I moved back from Austin . . . I needed a flexible schedule because of my mom, so he hired me."

"What's up with your mom?" Sandy couldn't help snooping. It's what he did best.

Chelsea shifted on their chair and looked away.

"Sorry. I can be rude and intrusive, and sometimes I forget that other people have boundaries."

They cleared their throat. "She has MS."

He put the pieces together. *They must be taking care of their mom, so that's why they moved back.*

Sam placed a highball glass of a bright red concoction in front of him and a frosted mug in front of Chelsea. She rested a hand on the back of Chelsea's chair.

Sandy lifted the glass and smelled cranberry. "What is this?"

"We call it a Kringle Cryer Cocktail. Pace yourself. Food will be up in a few." Sam squeezed Chelsea's forearm before she spun away to help a group that entered.

He took an exploratory sip of his drink and relaxed as soon as the delicious flavor hit his tastebuds. "You need to ask that girl out. Also, what the hell is in that mug?"

Chelsea flopped a hand at him about Sam. "Root beer."

Wrinkling his nose, he bent over to smell it when Chelsea held up their glass to prove they weren't kidding. "I've never met a grown adult that drinks that stuff willingly. Yeesh."

Chelsea gave a half shrug.

He sipped his drink. He couldn't stop wondering what had set Patrick off earlier in the day. "Any ideas who or what might have upset Patrick this afternoon? I thought he was going to rip the door off its hinges."

"Besides the super store and the financial issues, the only other thing I know about is his brother . . . "

Sam dropped off their food and turned away with a wave as more customers entered.

"This joint is crazy busy." All of the tables were full now, and the bar had people in every seat. "Something went down with his brother? Ooh, family drama. Can I have some more, please?" he asked in a horrible Cockney accent.

Chelsea chewed, setting half of their club sandwich down on their plate. Their brow rose as if questioning the idea of spreading rumors.

"I'm a horrible gossip. Get used to it and spill."

They wiped their mouth. "Dolan stole money from the store."

Surprised, Sandy flopped back in his chair. He didn't expect that at all considering Patrick seemed like a wholesome salt-of-the-earth type. He figured that kind of straight-arrow goodness ran in the McCormick family. Sandy grabbed his glass and chugged half the drink, completely disregarding Sam's warning. *It's mostly cranberry juice and it's light on the alcohol. What harm could it do?* "How did it happen?"

"How'd what happen?" Patrick materialized at the table with a beer in his hand.

Sandy's cheeks had already turned red from the alcohol, but now he'd bet they'd gone a scarlet at almost being caught digging for dirt about his boss. *Shit, did he hear that?*

CHAPTER 4

Patrick hovered at the table shifting his gaze between Chelsea and Sandy. He couldn't believe Chelsea would've shared anything about his brother and the money.

He rarely stopped in at Ace's, but today he needed to blow off some steam, and even though a workout would have done him some good he decided to take a night off and have a beer. These were the last two people he expected to run into.

"I didn't mean to interrupt. I can find a place at the bar." Patrick turned to leave, but Sandy caught him by the arm.

"Stay." He hopped off his seat and grabbed an empty chair.

Patrick accepted the seat with a half-smile. "Thanks." He turned his beer bottle around in concentric circles on the tabletop. For some reason, he was fidgeting. Probably because he'd barged in at an incredibly awkward moment. "You did great today. First day on the job and everyone loved you." Patrick sat up in his chair. "The *customers*. They really responded to you," he clarified.

"Be right back." Chelsea disappeared to the bar with their empty mug.

Sandy shifted in his seat as he chugged down the rest of his drink as if he needed to gather his courage. "Sorry about earlier. I kinda pried stuff out of Chelsea that I had no business doing, but I've been worried about you since this afternoon."

Gripping his beer bottle, Patrick wished he could say it was fine, but he didn't want to discuss his brother. Or the unpaid lease. Or the possibility of losing the store. Instead he asked, "Do you wanna play darts?"

His new employee reared back in near horror. "Only if you and everyone in this bar have a death wish."

"So that's a 'no'?"

Chelsea returned with fresh drinks for both men. "I have to head out. These are on me."

They bid Chelsea a good night and a nod of thanks.

"You two seem to be fast friends." Patrick slipped out of his chair and into Chelsea's. He could tell himself he'd made the move so he didn't have to keep thinking about crap he didn't want to think about, but honestly? He wanted to sit closer to his new photographer who smelled like peppermint and vanilla hair products.

"They're cool. And what can I say? I blend well with the

people." Sandy smirked as he leaned his head on his hand with a—what? Was that a flirtatious smile?

Patrick shook his head and finished the remains of his first beer.

"Although, it's kind of a commentary on rural Illinois that I'm the only Asian in this bar."

"You're the only Asian in this bar? What!" Patrick's shoulders started to loosen up and he couldn't help but enjoy staring at Sandy.

"Oh, so you do have a sense of humor hidden behind that usually sulky nature. Wonder of all fucking wonders."

Patrick blew out a puff of air, still not ready to talk about his sulky nature, but maybe he should offer something. "Wasn't at my best today," he muttered. "Sorry about that explosion earlier. That wasn't professional of me." His cell chirped from his back pocket. Relieved to have an excuse to move on, he pulled it out and looked at the screen. "Chelsea says check the weather."

Sandy slid his phone out of his jacket. "Holy crap. This can't be right. This kind of unexpected snow storm is unheard-of."

Patrick drummed his fingers on the tabletop. "What kind of vehicle do you have?"

"Prius. Why?"

Patrick's shoulders shook with suppressed laughter. *Of course, he does.* "Looks like you're stuck here."

The corners of Sandy's mouth turned up as he looked away for a moment. "Any Airbnbs around these parts?"

"Not a chance." Patrick sipped his beer. "You could . . . stay at my house."

Sandy's head whipped backward. His eyes held Patrick's.

Leaning his arms on the table, Patrick reminded himself that Sandy was an employee. "I have a guest room." He could have been wrong, but he swore Sandy deflated a bit at that information.

"Yeah, that'll work. I might have to raid your wardrobe because I have nothing with me. Do you have anything other than flannel? Oh, and Moonshine will need some food . . . Are you sure about this?"

He wagged a hand back and forth to let Sandy know he had his doubts about the offer, but it wasn't a big deal. He'd let the flannel dig slide for now. "Once the snow clears out, I can drive you into the city and you can get your stuff."

The brows on Sandy furrowed. "I'm not altogether helpless."

"Does your Prius have a big blade in the front for you to plow through this snowstorm? Or chains on the tires?"

Patrick thought the high-pitched squeak Sandy made as he looked at the ceiling was ridiculous and a little cute. "That's what I thought. You should think about staying in town while you're working at the store. It'd save you money, and you wouldn't be risking life and limb by traveling back and forth. My guest room is free if you want it. You're welcome anytime."

Sandy appeared to take a longer drink than normal. "I'll think about it. But only if you tell me what happened today."

Patrick wiped a hand across his face and hung his head

before downing his beer. He nodded at Sam across the barroom, requesting refills for them.

"Oof, it must be something horrible."

The weariness that had subsided now came roaring back. Hopefully, the beer would dull that soon. "We're being evicted." Patrick didn't know what possessed him to tell this stranger about the problems with the store. It wasn't like him to divulge confidential information so freely. Hell, his dad didn't even know yet. "I shouldn't have said anything . . ."

Sandy reached across the table and placed his hand over Patrick's. "Hey, who am I going to tell? Moonshine? Even if I did, she's like a vault." Sandy threw a thumb over his shoulder where Moonshine lounged.

Patrick welcomed the warmth of Sandy's hand on his. He couldn't help being amused at the joke. He could use more laughter in his life. The hair on his arm stood up. *I like him. No. Damn it. Employee.* He slid his hand out from under Sandy's.

Sam swung by and delivered their drinks. "These shots are on the house because it's taken me forever to clear your table." She scooped up the plates and debris and scooted away.

Sandy held up his shot glass and Patrick clinked his. Together they downed the Jameson.

Sandy's features twisted up at the whiskey. "And, you know, Chelsea's an extremely loyal friend to you, so if you did share this with them, I'd bet they'd be willing to brainstorm some ideas. And they're not the only one. The community really rallied this morning. One minute it was dead and then BOOM—packed."

Glancing around at the people in the bar, Patrick saw familiar faces. They didn't have to be here either, but they came out to put money back into the community to support one another collectively. Even if it was only for a beer or a soda, it mattered.

Sandy patted his hand. "The people in this town are amazing, which brings me to this: I took a ton of photos today. Let me plaster the site with them and post on social media."

That sounded reasonable, but Patrick's stomach turned at the idea of bringing the subject up to his dad. His dad's business ideals that were old fashioned. And these changes would have to be at both stores.

"Also, and this is a little bit bigger, but what if the community did a small business Saturday or whenever? It could be any day, but I'd think you'd want a weekend to really drive the sales. Maybe do virtual coupons, and there have to be hotels or something within decent driving distance so that people could come for the entire weekend or even overnight?" Excited at the idea, Sandy wiggled in his chair.

Patrick held a hand up to get Sandy to slow down on his plans. "Wait a minute. This would take a lot of coordinating with the town council and all our businesses. And even if we have the time to implement something like that before Christmas, I doubt the town has the kind of money required to put into an aggressive operation like this. We can't do something like this overnight."

Sandy made a slurping sound with his straw as he sucked the last of his drink from the very bottom of the glass. He inhaled a deep breath. "I'm getting ahead of myself. How about we pump things up online first? And save the idea of a small business plan for later."

These initiatives could be great for the entire community, but there wasn't enough time. Patrick downed the rest of his beer. The store was scrambling as it was, so an immediate sales boost is what he needed now. And the other thing was having this conversation with his dad. That would be a tough sell.

"Hey, I don't know about you, but these drinks are hitting me, and Moonshine looks tired. She worked her ass off today."

Patrick agreed with his drinking companion and headed to the bar for the bill.

"Wait. Let me Venmo you or give you some cash." Sandy stood to get his phone and wallet out of his various pockets.

Patrick shook his head. "We talked business. I can write it off."

Outside the bar, Patrick zipped his jacket up to his chin. The snow was really coming down now. He couldn't remember when they'd ever had a storm like this one.

"Where are you parked?" Sandy asked.

"My vehicle's at home. We're within walking distance."

Sandy moved to Patrick's right side with Moonshine. "Ah ha, you walk everywhere, don't you?"

"It's a fast commute. We just go down the street and then

through the park, and we'll be there." He pointed in the direction that they were headed.

"Do you seriously like living in a small town?" Sandy adjusted his earmuffs.

He dug his hands deep into his pockets. "Honestly, I never had much choice in the matter. It's the family business. The Mayfield location is the second one we opened. It kinda made me angry in the beginning, but then I got used to it. I was born in Madison, which is a college town, so I was raised on city energy. It took a while to acclimate to a rural setting. Slowing down and focusing on work and the people. Geez, this sounds pitiful."

"Not at all. And everyone loves you here and the store."

"My family's important to me, and making them proud is something that I want to do even as an adult." Patrick kicked a clump of snow out of the way for Sandy who smiled at the gallant effort.

"I get that. But didn't you feel like you were missing out on having fun?"

He gave a half-hearted shrugged. "I think I was always like this—responsible. Even in college, I went to class. I went to parties. I stayed in control." He glanced over at his walking partner. "I bet you were wild in college."

"Oh my hells, you don't even want to know." Sandy bumped him in the shoulder and a cheeky look crossed his features. "I bet you weren't boring and uptight *all* the time."

"Maybe not." Patrick bent down and scooped up some snow, tossing it at Sandy.

Sandy stopped in his tracks and dropped Moonshine's

leash. "Oh, it's like that, is it?" Sandy packed snow into a ball as Patrick ran ahead.

Maybe because of Sandy's sharp was of dressing, Patrick didn't think he'd be all that great at snowball fights, so he only put five feet in between them. As he turned to smirk, an icy missile hit him right in the forehead. Not one to be taken down by the first salvo, Patrick spun quickly and grabbed snow and pelted Sandy's shoulder. They went back and forth until both were out of breath.

Barking at the two men, Moonshine finally stopped beside Sandy, who gathered her leash.

Sandy joined Patrick on the sidewalk, Moonshine managed to run around them in a circle, tangling them in her leash. In one fantastical tug, Sandy lost his balance and fell on top of Patrick into a pile of snow.

Surprised, Patrick belted out a belly laugh as he held Sandy in his arms, while his heart ached as a feeling of longing fired through him.

Sandy's eyes widened and he joined in the laughter.

"I guess Moonshine wanted to win the snowball fight?" Sandy shifted his weight, moving himself up onto his arms.

Warm breath fluttered across Patrick's cheek. He needed to move quickly otherwise he feared he'd do something extremely stupid like kiss Sandy. "She doesn't fight fair." Patrick moved forward, accidently clunking Sandy's head.

They both winced at the contact.

Sandy rolled onto the ground next to him, rubbing his temple.

"Dog one, humans zero." Patrick blinked his eyes open

and closed. He bit the end of his glove, sliding it off his hand. Then he lifted the hair off Sandy's temple, inspecting the lump. The pink skin caused a tingle to run through him. "Are you good?"

Sandy winced. "You have a thick head."

Patrick put his glove back on and got to his feet. He held out his hand to Sandy. "That was fun."

"See, you know how to show a guy a good time." Sandy crinkled his nose up. "That sounded dirtier than I meant it."

"Although that's accurate." Patrick picked up Moonshine's leash and handed it to Sandy. The dog looked pleased with herself.

"And so modest."

Patrick shrugged. He couldn't stop a sly smile from appearing as they continued to move through the park. The snowflake shaped lights and giant decorated pine trees provided a magical glow on their trek.

Sandy spun around as they crossed a small bridge leading over a creek. "Is this place for real? I mean this is like some Thomas Kinkade-type dreamland. I almost can't believe it."

As they walked, Patrick took in his surroundings. It had been a long time since he really looked at the park and the decorations. The beauty of it all had been lost on him at some point. Seeing it through Sandy's eyes made him see how lucky he was to be in a place that celebrated the spirit of the holidays. "You're not hallucinating. Mayfield is a unique place during the holidays. It's been a while since I've been in Chicago in December. Do you have special parties and events to attend this time of the year?"

"Usually, I visit with my mom and step pop—get some food, exchange gifts. My best friend, Julia, and I normally go all out, but she's abroad this year. Parades, seeing the lights, ice skating—which is a massive mistake for my BFF since she's like Bambi on ice. Total hot mess. Although, the spiked hot cocoa afterwards helps. What we don't get is this peacefulness. The quiet. Anywhere you go in the city is noisy and jam-packed with people. It's nice getting away from that this year. How about you?"

"My family either comes down or I drive up to Wisconsin. It's always a half a day celebration because of our day post-Christmas sale at the stores. This year we're doing an employee dinner after the holidays. You should join us."

"Do I have to bring a dish to pass?" Sandy grimaced.

"Not a fan of cooking?"

"It's an either or with me—either it turns out or it doesn't."

Chuckling under his breath, Patrick retrieved his key from his jacket pocket. Sandy and Moonshine entered the picket fence's gate first. "Careful on that slick walk." The automatic outside light flashed on.

"Your house is beautiful. I love this classic brick with a hint of modern. The wood accents are to die for." Sandy's eyes shined brightly.

"Thank you. It took me a while to finish all the updates." Beaming at the compliment, Patrick stomped the snow off his boots on the welcome mat and moved to get the door.

"You're a man of many talents," Sandy's voice dipped low.

Patrick's chest lifted with pride. *Take it easy. It's a compliment not a marriage proposal.* Inside the foyer, he ushered Sandy and Moonshine into the house. He closed out the biting cold as quick as possible.

With a flick of a light, he made a sweeping gesture around the interior. "This is the open living room and kitchen. To the left, down that small hall is the guest room and bath. To the right of the kitchen is my room." Patrick slipped out of his jacket and hung it in the closet. He held out his hand for Sandy's jacket and stuff.

Sandy sat down on the little bench by the door and took off his boots, scooting them under the bench next to Patrick's. "Do you have a towel for her? She picks up all the snow."

Moonshine sneezed as if offended.

"Don't argue with me. You're like a mop."

With his hands on his hips, Patrick studied the two of them, delighted to have their company. *These two are something else. Adorable.* "Gimme me a second." He ran stocking-footed to his bathroom and dug out an old towel.

When he jogged back into the room, Sandy and Moonshine were waiting patiently. He handed the cloth over to Sandy who dried off Moonshine's do.

Bored and ready for action, Moonshine slipped out of Sandy's grasp and joined Patrick in the kitchen.

"I guess I was done drying her off," Sandy huffed. "Wow. This kitchen," he ran a hand over a countertop.

The exposed brick along with the stained cabinets gave the room a rugged look. A skylight above added natural light to the room, brightening the space.

Patrick grabbed a step stool and started opening cupboards. Slightly off balance, he wobbled. *I guess I had more to drink than usual tonight.*

Sandy came up behind him. "What are you doing?"

"Looking for the dog bowls." Stretching his arm out, he shifted stuff around in the back of the highest shelf.

"You had a dog?"

"Yup, an ancient labrador named Todd. He died a couple of years ago. I should've put him down before he got decrepit, but I didn't have the heart to do it. He used to come to the store with me every day. Mostly he'd snore in my office until it was time for us to go home." He balanced on his tippy toes and caught hold of the dishes. Sandy placed a steadying hand on his back. That tiny kindness and personal touch caused his pulse to pick up speed. Once his feet returned to solid ground, he came face to face with the guy who still had his hand on him.

Sandy's gaze roamed freely over Patrick like he was a peppermint stick he'd love to consume.

Without thinking it through, he followed his instincts, leaned forward and kissed Sandy. But just maybe it had something to do with how mesmerizing he looked standing in Patrick's moonlit kitchen.

CHAPTER 5

Sandy's hand balled tightly into Patrick's flannel button down. As Patrick cupped the sides of his face, he sank deeper into the heat and pine scent of the delicious man. Sandy stepped closer and rested his other hand on the jeaned hip of the lumberjack. The wiry beard rubbing against his face elicited a grunt of pleasure laced with pain.

As Sandy sank further into the moment, Patrick suddenly dropped his hands and stepped back. Wearing a tortured look, he bumped the step stool behind him and tipped it over. The loud crash broke whatever spell Sandy had fallen under.

"I shouldn't have done that."

Disappointed, and more than a little hurt, by Patrick's abrupt rejection, Sandy moved forward to stop him from—*what? I don't know.*

But it was too late. Patrick turned his back to him and

folded up the step stool, tucking it into a closet. "There are fresh blankets in the guest room, toothbrush and toothpaste in the bathroom. Excuse me while I get you something to wear."

Before Sandy could utter a word of protest, concern or disbelief, Patrick was gone, off to his room. Sandy frowned at Moonshine. "What the hell?"

Moonshine tilted her head.

"That's what I'm sayin'." Sandy leaned against the counter, too befuddled to go anywhere.

When Patrick returned, he barely came close enough to Sandy to hand over a pair of red and green flannel pajamas.

"I tend to keep it on the cooler side at night," he said from the edge of the kitchen. "Extra blankets are in your room."

"You said that already." He snatched the sleepwear from Patrick's out-stretched arm.

"Good night." Patrick practically stalked away, leaving an astonished Sandy in his wake.

Sandy shook his head as he led Moonshine to the guest room. He flipped on the overhead light and tossed the flannels onto the bed. Sandy couldn't figure Patrick out. *One minute we're flirting, then he's brooding, then the kissing, and then the one after that—what, we go separate ways? Who is he, Sybil?* Sandy turned on the bedside light and pushed the door closed with the back of his foot. He grabbed a couple of blankets from the closet, one for him and one for Moonshine and placed them at the foot of the bed.

Changing into the flannel, the scent of the fuzzy material reminded him of Patrick. "Is it his detergent?" He slipped into the pants and then the button down before performing his nightly rituals.

Patrick was right. The temperature of the house rivaled a meat locker. Sandy spread the blanket over the comforter on the queen bed and then snuggled in. He lay there blinking at the ceiling. This morning he had just met Patrick, got a seasonal job, and now he's here in the guy's home. This day was too much. He flipped the blankets off his body, ran to the chair, and retrieved his phone from his pants pocket.

Sandy hovered his finger over the FaceTime icon by Julia's name. It'd be so easy to call her right now. He needed to vent to his best friend, but he wasn't certain he had the actual energy for it, and saying that he'd made out with his new boss didn't really fit into her relationship plans for him. Not that it was her life, but something gnawed at him about Patrick. *What is it—I don't want him to be another notch? Ugh, that's what I need: a rural, flannel-wearing, brooding jock.* Instead, he texted her.

Hope your flight was good xoxo

Then he clicked open a search engine and typed in McCormick's General Store. The site was so lifeless and dull. On his Notes app, he started to type some ideas. It was doubtful that he'd get Patrick to change everything all at once, but at least he'd have an approach, a way to spruce it up. He genuinely wanted to help Patrick. The store meant so much to him. But of course, Sandy's hormones—or maybe the alcohol—made a betraying thumb press on the About navigation button.

Three members of the McCormick family popped up as the banner image. All of them were decked out in McCormick branded shirts. With her short curly hair, cheerful smile, and sweet round face, Patrick's mom looked like everybody's favorite mother from the heartland. McCormick senior resembled a beer-drinking sports enthusiast with his polo stretched over a beer belly. Whereas Patrick, with his rippling muscles and winning smile, sandwiched between his shorter parents looked like a model. The mysterious brother was missing in the promotional shots.

As he scrolled to the bottom of the page, Sandy's eyes nearly bugged out when he gawked at a photo of Patrick in his UW-Madison wrestling gear. *Ha! I knew it.* Somehow, when he'd first perused the site, he missed that photo. Although how he missed that tight unitard was a puzzler. The body hugging Lycra left very little to the imagination. *And I thought banana hammocks were revealing. Holy Guacamole.* Back in Patrick's college days he was much more defined with sculpted shoulders and a chiseled jaw, which irritated Sandy. How did he find the time to maintain that physique and attend his business classes?

Their college experiences were vastly different in that sense. Patrick skipped the party scene, and Sandy immersed himself in it. Even after he finished university—and to this day—he still loved going out and having fun. It didn't seem like Patrick's life consisted of anything outside of work. *How did he survive? How did he get laid?* Maybe that's why their kiss had freaked him out. Patrick was out of practice.

The next morning, Sandy awoke to the alluring smell of coffee and eggs. He rolled over and groaned. Moonshine hopped up on the bed. She stared Sandy down. "I really don't want to have to go out there and deal with mixed messages over bacon."

Moonshine tilted her head with one ear raised.

"Has anyone ever told you that you're annoying?"

Moonshine's bark refuted the opinion.

"Fine. We'll go, but I'm not giving you my bacon. You get kibble. Dry. Boring. Kibble."

Moonshine growled although she wagged her tail in triumph.

Sandy forced himself to get up, get dressed and face Patrick. He stopped at the front door for Moonshine to do her business.

Patrick's head popped around the corner from the kitchen. He waved. "Hi, there."

Sandy grunted a hello.

"Cream and sugar or black?"

"All of the above."

A moment later Patrick brought him a cup of coffee doctored with everything.

He blew on the life-affirming beverage before taking a sip. "Okay, good morning."

Patrick looked down and shook his head, but Sandy caught the slight smile. The lumberjack avoided Sandy and took a shaky inhale to say whatever he had to say. "I shouldn't have been so thoughtless last night. You're an employee and I want you to know that I didn't plan—"

To kiss me?

"To take advantage of you."

"You did?" Sandy tilted his head, pretending to have no idea what Patrick was talking about.

As if on cue, Patrick stopped studying the floor and mustered the courage to meet Sandy face to face. The dumb-founded look on Patrick's features shouldn't have caused such a thrill to surge though Sandy, but it did.

How long do I let him squirm? Is ten minutes too long? He basked in the chaos as he sipped his coffee for a minute. "I'm kidding."

A puff of air escaped, Patrick's lips. His broad shoulders lowered. "You're mean."

"Only when someone is being an asshat."

"I'm the asshat in this instance?" Patrick hooked a thumb toward his chest.

"Uh huh. I wanted to kiss you as much as you did me, so, you know, get over yourself."

"But in our business relationship I have the power—"

A bark from the other side of the door interrupted them. Sandy popped open the door wide enough for Moonshine to enter. "Oh please, Moonshine has the power. This girl's got all of us wrapped around her paws."

Worry lines creased Patrick's forehead.

"Relax, okay?" Sandy squeezed Patrick's shoulder. "You don't need to report yourself to HR. It was a consensual."

Patrick's winkles didn't disappear. But instead of continuing to discuss the matter, he grabbed the towel from the night before and dried off the dog. "Go help yourself in the kitchen. I got this."

Someone please, get the lumberjack to chill. But what if there's more to it? Is Patrick embarrassed? Sandy dragged his ass to the other room, fearing that he might be the reason why.

The table was set for two, and a nice spread was laid out with toast, scrambled eggs, bacon, fruit, and three different types of jam. He thought he died and went to breakfast heaven. *Patrick is so thoughtful. If he's really embarrassed of me, why would he do all this?*

Sandy snuck a piece of bacon off a plate. He moaned his approval just as Patrick walked into the room. "That sound wasn't for you. That's for my deep appreciation for a dead Porky pig and for the large quantities of fat that are clogging my arteries."

Patrick pulled a bag of dog food and filled Moonshine's bowl.

Nervous, Sandy crossed his legs to keep from bouncing them. "Where the hell did you get that?"

"I went for a run earlier this morning and picked it up at the gas station. Hope this brand is okay?"

They watched as Moonshine went to town on the food.

"Okay, if you're gearing up to reject me, you can stop romancing me with food." Sandy stuffed another piece of bacon into his mouth. "Also, running early in the morning? Who are you?"

A gradual smile graced Patrick's lips as he put the dog food away. He washed his hands and then sat diagonally from Sandy. He placed two large scoops of eggs on his plate and added a bunch of ketchup over them.

"Ah, you're that guy. The crazed condiment eater."

Patrick popped a piece of bacon in his mouth. "I don't really like eggs. I need the protein. And I'm not rejecting you."

"And you really like ketchup."

"And bacon and a lot of other stuff that's high in calories and fat."

Sandy speared fruit onto his plate. "And so you run to chase all of that away?"

"That and other things. I try." The strong man stuffed a forkful of the ketchup and egg concoction into his mouth with gusto.

As Sandy sipped his coffee, he studied the lumberjack over his mug. Patrick hadn't expanded on his rejected comment. Did that mean they were supposed to forget about the kiss and move on? Bothered by that idea, Sandy sat up straighter in his chair. "We need to talk."

A crease formed between Patrick's eyes as if he wasn't following the direction of the comment.

"Our chemistry. Specifically, last night."

Patrick swallowed and wiped his mouth. "Sure. The thing is . . . " He stopped and swallowed again. "The thing is . . . we just met. I'm your boss, and we don't know one another. I had a couple of drinks. And you're cute."

Sandy perked up at the idea of being called cute.

"But we have to work together. I didn't mean to overstep last night. Please accept my apology."

Patrick looked like he was waiting for Sandy's reaction, but he didn't have a clue what to do or say. *No rejection. No embarrassment. His weirdness is about work? Do I accept it and move on?* This was irritating. Something about Patrick's wooden words resembled a business arrangement. No, he didn't like this at all. "You didn't overstep—I liked kissing you. I've decided to take you up on the guest room offer."

Patrick's fork clanged against his plate. His raised brows and wide eyes caused a tickle of wicked delight to run through Sandy. *Oh yeah, big guy, I think we're gonna have an awful lot of fun together.*

————

Patrick shifted in his Santa chair. The store's florescent lights already pierced his eyes like ice picks, and it was only midmorning. The Santa suit made him especially itchy today, probably because he hadn't gotten any sleep last night. As he tossed and turned, he'd thought about the kiss. And then he'd thought about Sandy, alone in the guest room, and how easy it would be just to walk to the other side of the house. But he hadn't. He stayed in bed until he couldn't take it anymore, and then by four in the morning he'd had enough. Even though the temps had only hit the teens and it was slippery outside, he tied his running shoes, put on his winter gear, and braved the day.

Although, somehow, he didn't feel very brave. The word coward sprang to mind instead. But he'd been right to put the brakes on the kissing. They didn't know anything about one another, and just because Sandy was kind, cute, and funny didn't mean they should date. No, not date. The most he could handle was a fling. A holiday fling sounded just right. Some sweaty sex was what he needed. He didn't have time for anything more.

All his emotions and focus had to be on the store. His family was counting on him.

A throat clearing broke Patrick out of his reverie.

Sandy leaned a foot on the step. "It's really dead in here."

Patrick glanced around the store. They'd only had a couple of kids with their grandparents stop by for Santa photos so far. And there was all of one customer wandering around the first floor. Patrick hadn't seen anyone else enter the store since they opened.

Sandy pursed his lips. His very red, very kissable lips.

Sandy flagged a hand up and down in front of Patrick's line of sight. "Are you with me?"

He nodded. "Maybe take Moonshine and yourself for a break."

Sandy patted his leg and Moonshine followed him.

Patrick closed his eyes and rested his head against his palm. A wave of exhaustion hit him like a sledgehammer.

"Hey...are you alive?" Chelsea plopped down on the velvet footstool.

A grumbly sort of groan slipped out as he shrank into his chair. "If you couldn't work here anymore, what would you do?

Frowning, they folded their arms. "That's not cryptic at all."

He thought about telling them about the eviction notice. The sooner he told them, the sooner they could start looking for a new job. "I think we're going to have to close the store."

"Geez, that bad?"

Patrick made a crashing and exploding sound.

Chelsea's head shot back with raised brows. "You're being loopy." They placed their hands on their knees and leaned forward with a serious look. "If the store closes, I'd probably have to take a job at that new super store. I'd hate it. I'd hate the people. I'd hate the bright yellow vest they'd force me to wear. And I'd hate it when they'd screw up my pronouns. But mostly I'd hate it when they'd force me to stop coloring my hair. In essence, Mom and I would be fine, but I'd absolutely fucking hate it. What's the plan?"

Patrick leaned his forearms on his knees. "I really hoped you had one."

They took off their elf hat and scratched their head. "Use your resources."

"If I had any left—the bank can't help."

"The new guy."

"How can he help?" He sat upright at how happy it made him to think that Sandy might be able to help.

Sandy and Moonshine stepped onto the stage as he bit into a frosted Christmas cookie. "What's the haps now?" he asked as he chewed.

Chelsea raised a challenging brow at Patrick. Patrick knew that silent facial expression well. And currently he hated that stupid thing. And also loved it. Since he had no other options, he looked directly at Sandy. "I could use your help."

CHAPTER 6

For over four hours, Sandy and Patrick toiled in the office, going back and forth on the website design and creating a mock-up that could potentially potentially appeal to his father. Not that his dad was difficult. He was particular and his simple ways may have performed well when McCormick's was first starting out; however, the world and customers changed. The evolution of their online presence could meet with some resistance.

Sandy rounded the desk, holding out his phone with the new photos he'd added to the Mayfield store Instagram.

"This is amazing." Patrick scrolled, scanning through the celebration photos from yesterday.

"And we should do a countdown to Christmas. Like Twenty-Five Days Until and feature shots of sale items you'd want to push."

Patrick didn't like the sound of that because his dad

didn't approve of upselling. His style of old-school promo-tions tended to fall under the lowkey category. He squinted at the screen, wondering how to share that with Sandy.

"You hate that idea?"

Patrick leaned a hand on his desk bringing him closer to Sandy. "I like it. The hard sell is my dad." Sandy bit his lip, which almost made Patrick lose his train of thought. He blinked several times to snap himself back to the matter at hand. "It has to be a more subtle way of enticing customers for him to go for it. Not a go-go boy dancing in Santa's hat and a g-string on TikTok."

Sandy slapped the desk. "Now that's a marketing plan I can get down with." The troublemaker started to reach for his cell.

"Bad example." He held the phone out of reach. Sandy's breath danced over his neck and heat blossomed in Patrick's cheeks.

"Plus, I bet Papa McCormick isn't a fan of go-go boys. Ohhh, go-go girls are his thing, right?" Sandy grabbed Patrick's forearm and squeezed with giddiness.

"You're a terrible human being. I don't want to think about my dad and anything with the words go-go in it." He struggled to hold his laughter in.

"I dunno about that," an all-too familiar voice said from the doorway. "I always liked that Go Go Gadget fella."

"Dad . . . " Patrick's heart gave a sharp lurch. He couldn't believe his dad was standing in his office. He wore a big puffy green jacket with the store logo on it, jeans, and snow-covered heavy-duty Sorel boots. A lump formed in

Patrick's throat as if he and Sandy were caught in a compromising position. *Relax. You weren't doing anything.* "Mom texted that you guys weren't coming down. Is she here too?"

"We've got four-wheel drive. No big whoop. Where else would she be?" His dad stepped forward with his hand outstretched in Sandy's direction. "Pat McCormick, Senior."

Sandy's head whipped from Patrick to his dad. With his eyes bugged out, Sandy walked around the desk and took the offered hand.

"This is Sandy Holiday. He started working as our holiday photographer yesterday, but he's a professional with an impressive portfolio." His nerves kicked in with the unexpected visit. This wasn't like his parents. They didn't do surprise visits. They planned and communicated, almost to the point of annoyance. "Who's watching the store?"

His dad shrugged out of his jacket and hung it up like he intended to stay for a while. Then his mom buzzed in and beelined it behind his desk, capturing him in a hug. "Honey, don't fret so much. You'll get those wrinkles at the corners of your eyes. We have that nice young man watching it. You know him. Eric. His cousin wrestled with you at the UW."

Patrick exhaled as he hugged her. This was a typical response from his mother, full of vagueness and so and so's brothers-cousin-monkey-uncle. Once his mother let him go, she turned and snatched Sandy, hugging him, too. Patrick covered his face with his hands. There was no escaping this moment. No ripcord. No emergency ejector seat. He dropped his hands and went to hug his dad. "Sandy," he said over his dad's shoulder, "that intrusive woman squeezing you like a boa is Colleen, my mom."

Sandy stood to the side with a curious expression. He looked as if he'd spotted Santa and his reindeer flying through the air.

His dad helped Mom out of her coat and stashed it beside his own. "Store looks slow," he said to Patrick.

Sandy stepped forward. "Excuse me, um, Pat, but it is today. Yesterday was fantastic. Would you like to see some of the photos?" He inched toward Patrick's computer.

Patrick met him behind his desk, figuring he'd handle screen navigation while Sandy talked. He was relieved that Sandy was so personable and at ease with his parents.

"Let's go to Insta first," Sandy suggested.

He brought up a window on his browser with the store page on it.

"Aww, aren't they adorable? Look at those little ones." His mom cooed and tapped a finger against the Santa pics on the screen.

His dad jutted his chin out, determined to stay on topic. "How were sales yesterday?"

Patrick knew he'd ask. His dad always asked questions, and then he'd want to look at the receipts, numbers, and it went on and on. "We had a bump."

"There's not much staff here. Didja let them go early or something?" His dad chuckled at his own joke.

He hadn't told him about the staff cuts yet and hoped he could avoid that conversation until the new year. Apparently not. "I had to make some changes." Patrick didn't want to go into the intricacies in front of Sandy. The photographer knew a lot already, but as a new part-time employee he shouldn't know everything. And his dad caught on, but he didn't look happy. The crease between his eyebrows deepened as the silence stretched on.

Sandy clapped his hands together. "All right with that showstopper, maybe we could show him a few of the things we worked on today?" The kind man was trying to be helpful, but Patrick could feel the tension already building between his shoulders.

Patrick brought the mockup on the screen.

His dad took control of the mouse. Patrick didn't think the furrow in his dad's forehead could get any deeper, but there it was: a crack so deep that it looked broad enough to plant corn. And then his dad's nostrils flared. *Shit.* He swallowed, but his mouth was too dry. "Would you do me a favor and check in with Chelsea? Help them with whatever they need," Patrick said to Sandy, trying and failing to sound like he had a handle on things.

"Are you sure you don't want me to explain the redesign?" Sandy's features scrunched up as if confused by the request.

Patrick shook his head, trying to get him out of the room before his dad dismissed the work they'd spent half the day creating.

Moonshine bounced out of her makeshift bed and followed Sandy out the door.

Once they were gone, he didn't have to wait long for a response from his dad about the revamped site.

"What the hell is this?"

"Now Pat, give him a minute to explain." Mom jumped in to play defense for him.

"We don't have the money to go changing half a million things, nor do we have the time."

Patrick jammed his hands on his hips. "We don't need money to do these changes. Sandy has the marketing experience to play admin for us. He has some great ideas. We worked together this afternoon—just look at what we accomplished already."

Pat folded his arms and widened his stance. "Why the good god damn don't you have chairs in here? It's stupid."

"You know he does this to stay healthy. It's good for the heart." His mom rubbed his dad's shoulder in a soothing motion.

Dad rolled his eyes. "Is that why you hired this fella?"

"Not originally. But I think he's valuable as more than a photographer. Do you have an issue with him?"

His dad's mouth turned down. "He's not from here."

"Pish, neither are we. I like him. He smells delightful, doesn't he?" His mom chimed in, as if his scent was what made Sandy an integral part of the team.

"That don't explain why you think we need to be doing all this." Pat pointed at the screen.

"I've been sending you updates, but I've been sugar-coating things. Our situation's not good. We're not doing well at all . . . " Patrick inhaled a deep breath. He didn't want to say it, but he had to. It was time. "We need to consider a new plan for the Mayfield store. The overhead's too high. We're barely hanging on here."

His parents shared one of their nonverbal looks that said more than words. "But it could be slow from the storm, Honey."

"Not just the storm, Mom." Patrick shook his head vigorously, relieved to finally have this discussion. "Sales have been down for months. The unpaid rent along with that new super store opening early have compounded the problems. I don't know what else we can do other than boost sales through a grassroots type of marketing. This won't cost anything.'

"How the hell did it get this far?" his dad yelled. The veins in his neck pulsed and his face turned a dangerous shade of dark magenta.

———

After Patrick exiled him from the family meeting, Sandy found Chelsea in a storeroom on the first floor. They had a clipboard in their hands. "What's going on?"

Moonshine found a space out of the way and laid down.

"Toy drive. Count how many building blocks buckets are on that table." They pointed at a table next to them. When they looked up at him, they stopped writing. "You look weirder than usual."

Sandy moved the buckets around, counting. "I got kicked out of the meeting with his parents."

"And now you're pouting."

"Twenty-five." He blew his bangs out of his eyes. "If he'd let me stay, I could have explained things, but I got kicked to the curb."

They pointed at the next group of toys for Sandy to tally. He started counting and rearranging stacks of puzzles. "Most of the time I don't know what I'm doing, but I do know how to work the living shit out of social media, and I know how to take fanfuckingtastic photographs. These two things combined would be a Christmas miracle for this place."

"Is this your pitch to Mr. McCormick? Cuz it needs work." The dry remark wasn't lost on Sandy.

He slapped down a couple of boxes with unnecessary force. "Forty-two. Do children actually like puzzles? Children are fucking boring."

They gave a one-armed shrug. "Is all of this"—they moved their pen in a circular motion at him—"about being ousted from a meeting? You've been here only a day and a half."

"Ugh. Fine. We kissed."

Chelsea pursed their lips. "I did not need to know this."

"Now you do, so deal with it." Sandy slammed a puzzle down.

They tilted their head back. "I'm regretting this already . . . Was it bad?"

He shot them a deadly glare.

Chelsea held their hands up. "All right. Count the next pile and try to refrain from revealing any sordid details. I don't need any of that gratuitous nonsense clogging up my gray matter."

"Puhlease, you'd be lucky to hear of my exploits." He moved on to a pile of boxed footballs, which was exactly when it dawned on him that he'd enjoyed meeting Patrick's parents. In the past, he'd always sidestepped meeting parents or family or packs of friends. He liked to keep things casual. Simple. Easy. Disposable. *What the frickin' frack is happening to me?*

"It was lovely. The kiss. And it's messing me up in a way I've never been messed up before, which is hella bonkers. This tiny town and these damn pleasant people—how do you live like this? Twenty-five."

Chelsea made a mouth noise as they jotted the number down on their inventory sheet. "I can see how this is a trau-matizing experience for you."

He couldn't stop himself from rolling his eyes. Sure, he was overreacting, but he could be useful to Patrick and the store. And, maybe, he had a soft spot for the guy, too. "In Chicago, I have a simple dating routine."

They stopped writing and looked Sandy dead in the eyes. "A routine? For dating?"

"And it always works. It's casual and fun and easy. And now here I am in this teeny place sleeping over with the only other gay man in town, and for some inexplicable reason I don't think my usual is going to work, which chaps my ass."

Chelsea's shoulders shook and then a burst of laughter shot out of them. The uncontrollable laughter was so loud that Moonshine woke up from her nap and started barking along with the racket.

Sandy stood there with his arms folded. He leaned against

a toy-laden table and tapped his foot, waiting for the noise to die down.

Chelsea bent over, placing their hands on their knees.

"Are you good now?"

They stood, pinching their side.

I hope that cramp doesn't go away all day.

"You know nothing about relationships," Chelsea accused. "You've never even had one."

Sandy snatched their clipboard from them. "I'm sick of counting. And I don't even know why we're talking about relationships. I don't want one."

A smirk crossed Chelsea's lips as they moved to a pile of teddy bears. "Who're you trying to convince?"

He tapped his pen against the clipboard. He liked his relationships. They were fresh and new and always extremely exciting. Plus, big bonus: they were always hot and sweaty. *Who didn't love a night full of sex and no sleep?* But when he thought about Patrick it wasn't only about the physical, but a warm Christmas cookie feeling happened, too. This was all Julia's fault. "Maybe I want to spend more time with Patrick, and maybe I want to get to know him. Why do I feel dirty?"

Chelsea snatched their clipboard back from Sandy and wrote down more toy totals while he was in his pensive state. "It sounds like what you're having are what we humans call emotions."

"You know if I weren't a big-hearted gentleman I would run over to the bar and tell that fun-sized Latina that you have the hots for her."

Chelsea's back went rigid, and they stood up to their full height.

Sandy tilted his head back, looking up at her. "Heh, I have a big mouth. I say stupid things. Don't crush me. Please."

The corners of their mouth rose, and they sat on the edge of a table. "You're scared. Of Patrick."

He tilted his head side to side. "It's different. The big thing is that he's not interested. Maybe he is. Okay, he is, but he's my employer."

Chelsea pulled out their phone and texted and then put their phone back in their pocket. "Had to ask the nurse to stay late with my mom," they explained. "We're almost done here. Want to hang after? If you quit annoying me then maybe I could help you with this issue you're having with Patrick."

"I'm shocked you actually want to. I get this general feeling of indifference from you." Sandy rested a fist on his hip.

"You're not wrong." Chelsea pointed at a stack of coloring books for Sandy to inventory.

"Ugh, I really, really like you." He smirked as he resumed counting. Sandy didn't know why, but he was fairly certain they'd just crossed over the from acquaintances to friends. *And maybe they could help me figure out how to manage that same step with Patrick.*

————

In a surprising turn of events, after a burger and veggie burger, Chelsea still wasn't sick of him. They offered to drive him and Moonshine to Chicago to pick up some essentials. They, like Patrick the night before, didn't think he should risk driving his Prius. Obviously, neither one knew that the compact vehicle could handle tough conditions, but Sandy let it go.

"Keep spending time together," they offered.

Sandy gave them a droll look even though their eyes were on the road. "That's your magical answer for us to get closer."

"Sometimes simple is best."

Sandy wanted to smack them in the forehead. "Now you're sounding like a fortune cookie. Maybe don't help so much."

On their way back to Mayfield with Chelsea's truck stuffed to the gills, they took an exit Sandy didn't recognize.

"Are you taking me to a remote area to chop me into tiny pieces?"

Chelsea's evasive shrug didn't put him at ease.

"Fantastic. Although, I will put up a fight, because I haven't seen the end of this season's Drag Race."

They shook their head. "I'm curious about the super store. And there it is: our worst enemy."

Transfixed, Sandy stared out the window. "Holy jingle balls, this place is gigantic. It's like a Costco-ate-a-Sam's-Club. It's disgusting." And yet, secretly, he loved it. A giddy sensation ran up his spine. Sandy loved warehouse stores. It was his mother's fault for teaching him to worship buying toilet paper in bulk.

As Chelsea drove through the parking lot, checking out the exterior, Sandy spied a Coming Soon sign with *A Subsidiary of the Lance Right Corporation* tag written beneath the store name. A flicker of recognition flared in his mind. *Oh no. Please, please, please let me be wrong.* He pulled his cell phone out of his pocket and scrolled through his emails. His hand froze over a recent message, and he vomited a little in his throat. Right there in black and white was his contract for his gig in the new year. Product placement photos for a Lance Right Corporation. *Fanfuckmylifetastic. I'm working for the enemy.*

CHAPTER 7

When they arrived at McCormick's store, Sandy cleared off the snow from his car and he and Chelsea went their separate ways. The odd thing was that driving to Patrick's house took longer than walking since the road that led to his home wound all the way around the park. When Sandy pulled up to the house, another car was taking up space in the driveway. Patrick's parents. Sandy draped his arms over the steering wheel and rested his forehead against them. *Why didn't I think of this earlier? How do I face them? And now I'm going to have to drive all the way back to Chicago when I'm dead tired.*

A knock on his passenger window made Sandy's head pop up. Patrick stood outside in a UW sweatshirt and jeans, with his hands tucked in his pockets. Sandy hit the automatic window. "I should go back to Chicago."

"Nah, let me in," Patrick said as he shivered.

Sandy popped the lock on the doors and pushed the button to make the window go up. "I didn't even think—really, I can go. It's not a big deal."

Patrick placed his hands in front of the vent, rubbing them together. "Don't be silly. My parents have the guest room, and I can take the couch."

"What?! No. If anyone is taking the couch it's me."

"Not on your life. If my mom sees you on the furniture in the morning, she'll yell at me. And I mean yell. She might be short in stature, but the woman can project her voice. She sings in her church choir. Trust me, you don't want to witness that. Animals run from that." Patrick smiled and turned to scratch Moonshine behind the ears when the dog popped her head between the seats. "If we're arguing about this, then you're staying?"

Moonshine barked in approval.

"You're the most unhelpful animal I've ever known." Sandy inhaled a deep breath. "We'll stay. But if I get in your way or your parents', then I'll skedaddle on out of here."

A flick of Patrick's hand brushed the idea away. "Pop the trunk so I can help you with your stuff."

As soon as Sandy hit the trunk release on the key fob, Patrick was out the door. "If this goes south, I'm selling you to the lowest bidder," Sandy muttered to Moonshine, who countered the threat with a sneeze.

Sandy grabbed the dog and her bed from the floorboard. They trekked up the path to the house behind Patrick who, naturally, carried all of Sandy's things with the ease of a pack animal. He had to admit that Patrick's muscles were exceptionally handy. Sandy squeezed himself in front of Patrick and swung open the door for him.

"My parents already hit the hay. They're early risers." Patrick's voice dipped low as he popped his boots off while balancing Sandy's stuff. He headed to his room.

Sandy unraveled his scarf and hung up his things before toweling off Moonshine. He was staying at Patrick's. Patrick who didn't know that he worked for the company that could essentially put him out of business. *Why does this kind of stuff always happen to me?* At that moment his phone buzzed from his back pocket. He looked at the text from Julia.

> Tokyo is cool. So tired. Feel free to FT when you're available. Hope the elf gig is going well. Xoxo

It's almost as if she can sense the chaos from abroad. And if matters couldn't get any worse, he was going to take Patrick's bed. Sandy unclipped Moonshine's leash and hurried toward the primary bedroom. He couldn't take the bed. He'd lose his mind if he had to deal with his job secret and kicking the man out of his own room. *Nope. That's not going to happen.* As Sandy crossed the threshold, he stopped dead in his tracks.

Patrick turned, shirtless. "Thought I'd change into pajamas."

Sandy closed his mouth with a snap. He may or may not have made some sort of mouth noises, but he wasn't certain they were words. Sandy shook himself back to the moment and placed the doggie bed in a corner. "I really can't let you sleep in the living room. So . . . um, you need to sleep here. In bed. You sleep in bed. With me." *What's wrong with me? Who talks like this?*

Patrick slipped a Henley over his head.

Oh, thank Santa he covered up.

"Deal." Patrick unbuttoned his jeans.

In a panic, Sandy nodded as he searched the room for his bag. He needed to not be in the same vicinity as Patrick when his pants came off. "Point me to my bag?"

Patrick pointed to Sandy's bag on a folding luggage rack. He popped it open and grabbed his toiletries and pajamas. "I shall return." He zipped into the bathroom like roasted chestnuts hit him in the butt.

Sandy rested his palms on the countertop and closed his eyes. First, he concentrated on pushing the image of a bare-chested Patrick from his mind. But the problem was that his double-crossing brain decided to flash images of him mapping that territory with his mouth. The only way to fix this was with a very cold shower. And seeing as the house was already as cold as the North Pole, this would ensure that he froze all thoughts of the shirtless Patrick from his mind.

Sandy flipped the knob to start the shower and stripped down in record time. He hopped in, "Fuck!"

A knock came from the door. "Are you okay?"

"Fine." Sandy shouted back. "Just freezing my guilty ass off," he mumbled to himself.

"The water takes a while to warm up. Do you need anything?"

"Nope. All good." Sandy grabbed his body wash and started to go through his routine. *How am I going to tell Patrick about my job with the Lance Right Corporation?* Although he didn't even know if he should. Technically, he wasn't working for them yet. But he couldn't quit the job. The last time he was in serious financial debt he'd sold photos to TMZ, which hurt Julia and her sister. *I'll never do that, again.*

He needed a stable job with health and dental benefits. He hadn't had that kind of security in years and the pay. The pay was amazing. Plus, the product placement gig would diversify his portfolio. Yeah, he couldn't pass on the job.

By the time Sandy stepped out of the shower he was no closer to a solution. As he performed the rest of his nightly routine, his nerves kicked in as he realized that he was about to sleep with Patrick. Well, not sleep, sleep, but actually close eyes and count sugar-plums. The handful of times he'd done this with other men it was usually after sex, which was different in this situation. There'd be no sex. "What the hell do people do in bed if they don't have sex?" he asked his reflection in the mirror. *Sleeping shouldn't be this stressful.*

He hung his towel up and squared his shoulders. *It's sleep. No biggie.* Sandy opened the door.

Patrick was already in bed reading a book. A lamp on the nightstand created a warm glow to the room and the handsome man.

Sandy crossed to his side of the bed. "Whatchya reading?"

Patrick held the book up.

"Blake Crouch. *Upgrade.*" Sandy pulled back the duvet and sheet and slipped under the covers. He adjusted the pillows behind his back before settling in. "Did you read *Dark Matter*?"

"That's my favorite."

Sandy smiled at the fact that they liked the same book. "I, ah, have a confession."

Patrick placed a bookmarker between the pages and turned his full attention to Sandy.

"I've never really slept in a bed with a guy I haven't had sex with, so this is super crazy weird for me. Like, what's the protocol?"

Setting his book on the table, Patrick balled one of his pillows, and stretched out on his side, facing Sandy. "I guess maybe don't steal all of the covers?"

Sandy turned to face Patrick too. He kind of liked this intimate bubble they were creating. "Covers. Okay."

"No kicking."

"Uh huh. I can do that."

"No hair pulling,"

Sandy knitted his brows together. *That's odd.* "You're full of shit."

The corners of Patrick's mouth rose. "Yup."

"I might want to kick you."

Patrick snorted. He turned and clicked off the bedside lamp. "There are no rules," he said.

Through the soft, moonlit room, Sandy could see the contours of Patrick's face. His breath hitched. Sandy didn't know how he felt about the "no rules" rule. If he closed the distance between them, Patrick might reconsider his no-rule thing or maybe he wouldn't. Sandy needed to stop torturing himself. A change in subject was a good idea. "Do you get along with your parents?

Patrick shifted in the bed as if he'd rather not talk about his folks. "Most of the time but working together makes things more complex. If you had to work with your folks all the time, how would you feel?"

"First off, I could never work with step pops. He's a boring man of epic proportions. And my mom . . . I love her something fierce, but absolutely not."

"And add into the mix a brother who steals from the store. I don't advise anyone to ever work with their family if they know what's good for them."

"Then why do it?"

Patrick wiped a hand over his face and groaned. "Kinda don't know anymore."

Maybe this was a good thing. Patrick wasn't happy at his job, so Sandy working for the enemy might not be as horrible as he thought. *Yeah. Sure. That's wishful thinking.* "Seriously, what would you do if you didn't have the store anymore? First thing that comes to mind. Go."

"I'd be an athletic coach." Patrick covered his mouth. "Woah, I didn't know that."

"See. This is what happens when you allow yourself to want things . . . " Sandy hadn't meant for the subtext to slip out, but there it was in all its glory for Patrick to hear.

Patrick sighed. "It's not that I don't want. I do . . . want . . . "

And Sandy wanted something, too, but that would make things even more complicated. Maybe it was a better idea to stay away from that sticky conversation. "How about something easier? Why wrestling? Isn't that kind of gay?"

"Repressed homosexuality. Haven't heard that before," Patrick chuckled. "It's a great sport, and I had a lot of pent-up energy. And I used sports as a way to expend it. Plus, I love sports."

"Ugh, you're one of those guys who watches it on the weekends, aren't you? Reliving your glory days." Sandy couldn't stop himself.

"If I had the time, but the store . . . " Patrick shrugged. "I like participating more than watching. Speaking of work, we're going to move ahead with your upgrade to the site. It took a lot of convincing, but I think Dad gets it now."

Without thinking, Sandy squeezed Patrick's muscular arm. Or tried to. *Damn, that's one hard bicep.* "That's terrific news. I'll get started on it tomorrow. And I know this is going to sound cray, but I think Chelsea would be great on TikTok for the store."

Patrick's features scrunched up.

"They're young with a dry sense of humor and they're edgy. It might be a good idea to tap into the youth market." Sandy stopped himself. It was too quiet. "What? What is it?"

"This is a great idea. It's just, I dunno. I mean with everything online could we get that demo? Most of the time it's thirty-five and up for our store. Sure, kids come in with their parents, but that's the extent of it. The younger market doesn't willingly come to our store."

"Have you tried targeting them before?" Sandy accidently grazed Patrick's chest. "Isn't it worth trying?" *Do not think about those defined pecks.*

The mattress dipped as Patrick rolled closer causing their

arms to touch. A tingling sensation ran through Sandy like an electric current.

Patrick didn't budge. In fact, he seemed content to stay connected to Sandy. "My dad wants us to attend the opening of the box store."

"No. That's not smart. Why would you? It's the competition. They're evil. Bad. And again, no." He stumbled, uncertain if it was because of the conversation or the warmth of Patrick's body.

"If I really thought we could compete with them then it'd make more sense, but I think he's worried and curious. That place does bulk. And I think they'll even have a service station. Customers will be able to get their tires rotated and oil changed while they shop. That's out of our league."

"Yes, see, no reason to go." Sandy wasn't completely relaxed yet. He didn't want Patrick to go to that super store. For some reason, it was too much of a risk if he did.

Patrick rested a hand on Sandy's thigh. "Aren't you curious?"

Yes, I'm curious. Curious how I'm going to sleep next to you all night. Ugh. "Not at all." Sandy hoped to put a pin in this conversation.

"Maybe I'll ask Chelsea to go with me. They'd like to see it, I bet." Patrick squeezed Sandy's thigh.

Son-of-a-Christmas-cookie. "I'll go. I don't think it'll be anything special. It's another warehouse full of stuff. Nothing I haven't seen before."

If Patrick and his parents were going, then he was going with them to play chaperone. It was the only way he could control the situation. Well, maybe not control it so much as prevent anything from happening. Not that it could, right? He didn't know anyone at the store and why would they know a random product photographer? The only people he knew were the HR folks and the product people from the corporate office. It would be fine.

Once Patrick removed his hand, Sandy released the breath he'd been holding.

"I'm glad you're coming. Besides photography and decent taste in books, what else do you like to do?"

"I watch way too much TV. I might actually have a problem because I love it that much. My best friend, Julia, and I attend Drag Race nights at our local watering hole. Oh, and I can't live without music and dancing."

"Your best friend's a girl? She's going to give you cooties." Patrick smirked.

"Yeah, yeah, yeah, I have a female best friend. I don't care what people say—adults can have BFFs for life. And I do, so there. You're just jealous."

It could have been his imagination, but he was pretty sure that Patrick intentionally snuggled his feet with Sandy's.

"I'm definitely green with envy. Maybe because this Julia character gets to hang with you."

Awe, he's so sweet. A warmth spread through Sandy's chest and into his manly bits. "I dunno, we're slayin' this job of chilling together."

"How'd you get into photography?" Patrick yawned.

Sandy saw Patrick's lashes blink like they were made of

lead. "My mom encouraged it after my bio dad bolted when I was a kid."

"That's rough. Do you see him much?" Patrick closed his eyes.

"Nope, he lives somewhere in Korea or wherever. I say good riddance. His crap parenting skills and disrespecting my mom put an icicle through our relationship a long time ago. After he was gone, she gave me one of her old cameras, motivating me to look at the world around me."

"Good mom."

Sandy couldn't stop his mouth from turning up at the heavy-eyed Patrick. "We should go to sleep," he whispered.

"Not tired," came Patrick's warm minty response.

Sandy kept his gaze on Patrick until the man's breathing evened out. He slipped out of bed, carried his phone to the bathroom and closed the door. From the edge of the bathtub, hit the FaceTime icon, ringing Julia.

Her faced popped up on the screen. She wore a backpack as she moved through a market on the other side of the world. "I thought the town of Mayfield ate you, or you got stuck in a tree looking for WiFi service. What did I miss?"

"Besides my face?" Sandy crossed his legs, hoping to retain some warmth as he spoke in a low tone.

"That's a given. Seriously. Why are we whispering?"

"I don't want to wake up—let's not talk about that. I have a problem. The big job in the new year is conflicting with my current gig. How the hell do I fix this hot mess?"

Julia stopped walking. "Really? You're calling me for

career advice? This is very unlike you, and now my concern is drifting into worried territory . . . I'll need more details."

Sandy dropped his face into a palm. "The people are so nice. I don't want to hurt anyone."

"Yeah, now I'm full-blown worrying. You despise nice people. And you seem okay wounding a lot of your hook-ups. Downright nasty a few of them were."

"Okay, okay, I don't need a play-by-play on the ghost of hot bodies past. How do I do this whole get-what-I-want and not, you know . . . "

Throwing her head back, she laughed. "Have your cake and eat it, too? If you want the cliched version."

"Uh huh, that thing. I want that." He nodded. "This tiny store in this fucking picturesque town is struggling, and my boss is going to lose his store to corporate overlords."

"The lumberjack?"

"Yeahuh, so, hi creative person—spitball some ideas at me to save it."

A sly smile crossed her features as she resumed strolling. "You like this guy."

He snapped his fingers at the phone.

"Um, GoFundMe," she blurted as her eyes focused on something off camera. "Noodles." Julia detoured.

"Jingle my bells! We can raise money for the store."

Julia nodded, focusing her attention elsewhere.

Sandy sat upright. *Maybe I'll be able to sleep tonight with Patrick and not feel like a shady Grinch after all.*

CHAPTER 8

The next morning, Patrick woke up with his arms full of Sandy. He blinked a few times to get his bearings. This wasn't good. *You tell Sandy you can't get involved with him, and then you go and snuggle him in your sleep.* He covertly pulled his arm out from behind Sandy's neck, unwrapping himself from the cuddly body that seemed to fit him just right. As he shuffled off the bed and stood, he glanced down at his pajama pants. Yeah, he was interested in Sandy more than as a friend. At least that's what his dick was telling him.

With fresh clothes in hand, Patrick headed toward the shower. Once the cold water hit him, he woke up for real. He calmly breathed in and out, waiting for his arousal to subside.

Would it really be so bad if they tried dating? Sure, he was Sandy's boss, but it was only a seasonal job. If he could assure his dad the relationship wouldn't have an effect on their workday, then everything would be fine. Or he could not tell his dad and just ask Sandy out anyway.

If he were being totally honest, he'd admit that his dad didn't want to know about his dating and personal life.

Sure, he came out years ago, but it seemed as if his dad never accepted it. They didn't talk about it; sweep it under the rug is what Pat, Sr. did when it came to his son's sexuality.

Patrick wanted to be the bigger man and let it go, but it didn't seem fair. His dad was proud of him for so many things in his life—wrestling, business, and strength—why not love?

His mom was the opposite. She asked questions and joined PFLAG. She even gave him suggestions on his Grindr profile, which should have been embarrassing, but secretly he loved how excited she got when she looked at his finished profile.

But when Patrick asked her if she ever thought his dad would go with her to a PFLAG meeting, she turned silent. *Maybe I should just tell mom about Sandy?*

He stepped out of the shower and toweled off. He couldn't believe he'd only known Sandy for a couple of days. When they were together, conversation flowed so easily. And, okay, yeah, his mom was right, Sandy smelled incredible. *He's handsome, funny, and invested in helping me save the store.* In a way, Sandy was his Christmas miracle. He shook his head. *This guy is making me sound cheesy.*

Patrick decided to ask Sandy out. If things went well, he'd tell his mom. She wouldn't tell his dad, but she'd probably encourage Patrick to share the news with him. Patrick knew it was a good idea to keep telling his dad about his life, but it was always so difficult, and it never made him feel happy. It made him feel ashamed. Patrick sighed as he dressed.

When he got to the kitchen, his mother had commandeered the stove along with his dad. They had pancakes in the works with bacon and sausage sizzling on the griddle.

"You didn't have to make all this." Patrick brought a mug down from the cupboard and poured himself some coffee.

"Honey, it's not a problem. You should wake Sandy. He won't want to miss breakfast." His mom flipped a pancake.

Patrick poured a second cup for his overnight guest. If yesterday was an indication of how Sandy felt about mornings, then he assumed coffee would be mandatory. He carried the cup into the bedroom and set it on the nightstand. He gave Sandy's arm a squeeze. "Hey, Mom wants to know if you're going to come eat with us."

"How is it morning already?" He sat up with his hair sticking out all over the place.

"We didn't go to bed that late."

Sandy yawned.

He passed the mug of coffee to Sandy.

The barely awake man, sipped, making a groan at the back of his throat then muttered, "Laptop."

"I need a few more words than that."

Sandy gave him an affectionate look. "Last night I stayed

up working on something, so grab your laptop from the chair."

Patrick grabbed the computer. "What am I looking for on it?"

When Sandy made a 'gimme' motion Patrick slid into bed next to him.

As Sandy clicked into a browser, Patrick wiggled closer to see what he was up to. The GoFundMe page for McCormick's General Store stared back at him.

"It's not live, yet," Sandy cautioned. "I'd like to add a video of you and some shots of the store. I wrote up a sample script last night, but it's subject to your approval."

Stunned, he stared at the page. Again, this man surprised him with his initiative and concern for the store's welfare and future. Patrick turned to look at Sandy. "You're amazing."

Sandy beamed at the compliment.

"Thank you—I never would have come up with this."

Sandy waved his hand in the air. "I don't buy that. Eventually, you would've been brainstorming and come up with something. This won't solve all the financial stuff, but it's a start."

"After we go to the box store groundbreaking, we can get started on the video and then announce the campaign."

Sandy's brows squished together. "Are you sure I should go? Maybe I should be at the store?"

Patrick got out of the bed. "Chelsea's got it. They've filled in before. Besides, I want you there. You see things much more creatively than I do."

"Oh, I see. You're using me for my brain. This is a first."

"You know you're awesome. Now get a move on."

Sandy hopped up. "Aye, aye."

Patrick smirked as he placed his laptop on the kitchen table. "Hey, I need to show you two something."

His parents turned off the stove, carrying over platters of pancakes, bacon and sausage, along with a big bowl of fruit.

His mom wiped her hands on a towel as she took a look at the device.

"A great idea to help save the store," she said, immediately on board.

His father stared at the screen in horror. "This makes us look like a charity case. That's not what we are. Take it down."

In defiance, Patrick placed his hands on his hips. "First of all, it's not live." This time he needed to put his foot down. It was a good plan, and it wouldn't cost them anything. "And secondly, no. We need other sources of income. We can't rely upon customers coming into the store. We need everyone to notice us, and this campaign can do it. I know you hate change, and you never had to deal with outside money in the past, but this isn't thirty years ago. Our stores didn't have online competition. And box stores weren't as common as they are today."

A fully dressed Sandy stepped into the room. "It's all right to be scared of something like this, but is it scarier than losing one of your stores?"

Dad crossed his thick arms over his chest. "I don't want this to harm the brand. We're a mom-and-pop shop, not a conglomerate."

"Dad, a fundraising campaign doesn't hurt us. It'll help us, hopefully, to keep our heads above water until we figure out a longer-term solution."

Reluctantly, his father took a seat at the table. He stabbed a few pancakes off the plate. "Let's eat."

Patrick stalked off with his laptop. He wanted to yell. Why did everything always have to be an argument and a fight to prove that he knew what he was doing? When would his dad trust him enough to listen and approve of his plans?

―――――

They all piled into Patrick's SUV for the trip to the box store. Sandy couldn't handle the deafening silence between the two McCormick men, so he dialed around in desperation and found a Christmas pop station on the radio. Sia's "Candy Cane Lane" and Ariana Grande's "Santa Tell Me" helped pass the time.

Thankfully, the drive didn't take long. Sweat rolled down Sandy's back. This was like strolling into the Grinch's cave, and it felt as if he were Max, the poor dog who basically gets smacked for being a loyal companion. Not that they were companions, but he could relate to that foolish animal. He wasn't certain what would happen during this visit. It stressed him out just thinking about stepping a foot into that store.

As the vehicle turned into the busy parking lot.

"Not as many people as I thought there'd be." Patrick pulled into an open spot near the building.

"Who are you kidding? They're busy," his dad grumbled.

Patrick released his seat belt with a snap and got out of the SUV.

Sandy hurried after him, following as he zig-zagged through the standing crowd. Patrick was leading them as close to the ribbon-cutting as possible. Evidently, he needed to look the enemy in the face. Sandy reached out and caught his jacket sleeve. "This is good enough. Your parents haven't caught up to us."

Patrick spun around. "Don't worry about it. They'll find us." Patrick's nostrils flared. It was obvious he was still upset with his dad.

"Do you want me to talk to him?"

Patrick shook his head. "Not a good idea. Let's just get closer."

Sandy sighed. What else could he do but follow? He made his way through the crowd and stopped when he almost ran into Patrick's back at the front of the onlookers. *Why does this feel like I'm just asking for trouble?*

The store manager stepped up to the microphone to begin the festivities. Probably due to the chilly weather, the store leaders and corporate representatives kept the speeches short and cut the ribbon. Everyone flooded into the building, helping themselves to hot beverages and finger foods, all items sold at the box store. Sandy followed Patrick as he made his way to the manager and the other corporate goons.

"How does it feel to put small businesses in our community out of business?" Patrick snapped at the bald man with Art on his name tag.

"Ah, well . . . I didn't get your name." Art clasped his hands together in front of his crotch—the international sign of fearful assholes everywhere.

"Patrick McCormick. McCormick's General Store in downtown Mayfield."

One of the female corporate stooges took that moment to point at Sandy. "Do I know you? Your face is awfully familiar."

Sandy squinted at the woman, trying to place her. He was sort of certain that they had met at the corporate headquarters. He shrugged. Nonverbal denial was best in this situation.

Art adjusted his glasses and turned to two employees. "Mr. McCormick has the shop in the three-story building." Art pivoted back to Patrick. "We're growing the economy for a brighter future for your community. What we offer here at PriceCo will provide consumers with items unavailable at your store. Additionally, if you and your staff open yourselves up to a new opportunity, working for Lance Right might be in the cards—especially for a manager such as yourself."

Sandy turned to see Pat Sr barreling toward Art. "You no good son-of-a—"

Sandy and Patrick managed to stop Pat before he had a chance to take a swing at the guy. Patrick's mom held onto her husband's jacket, trying to stop him. The heavy man made a lot of ground as he tried to get to Art, dragging them all in his approach.

Grunting, Sandy struggled to hold Pat's arm. "You should run," he said to Art, as he adjusted his grip on Pat's arm.

"Dad, calm down."

Pat's red face turned purple. Sweat covered his face. One minute they were trying to block him from attacking a man, and the next, they were trying to hold him steady.

"I think somethings wrong with your dad," Sandy told Patrick. "Call 911," he told Colleen.

"Oh my goodness," she said with the phone already in her shaking hand.

Sandy helped lower Pat to the floor. Patrick unzipped his dad's jacket. He could hear Patrick's mom providing disjointed information to the emergency services operator.

"Dad?" Patrick squeezed his dad's hand.

"My hands are tingling." Dad mumbled.

Sandy stood and placed an arm around Patrick's mom, comforting her. Colleen shook with worry. He murmured a few soothing words to her, which seemed to work as the trembling stopped.

One of the corporate employees handed Patrick a blanket to place around his dad.

They didn't have to wait long until the EMTs rolled onto the scene. They got Pat on the gurney and pushed him toward the door. Patrick walked with Colleen until she was tucked inside the ambulance with Pat.

As the ambulance drove away, Sandy held an open palm out to Patrick. "Give me your keys."

Patrick's features twisted up as if he were on the verge of tears. Sandy hugged him. "He'll be okay."

Patrick cleared his throat and stepped back.

As they walked to the SUV, Sandy held Patrick's hand. He'd never been in a medical situation this scary before. Feeling the warmth of Patrick's hand in his caused a sweeping rush of affection to gather in his chest. He was here for Patrick, and Patrick appeared to like having him around, too.

CHAPTER 9

At the hospital, Patrick paced the waiting room floor. Without having to check, he felt Sandy's eyes following each step. Ever since his dad started having issues, Sandy had stayed close. Just having him nearby was a relief, but he'd been helpful in other ways too. While he and his mom fretted, Sandy somehow kept his own energy under control, brought snacks, and entertained them.

A middled-aged woman wearing a lab coat with a stethoscope draped around her neck cleared her throat in the waiting room door to gain their attention. "Pat McCormick's family?"

Patrick held his hand in the air and slid into the seat beside his mother. He placed a comforting hand on hers.

"I'm Dr. Gupta. I've been looking after Mr. McCormick."

"How's my father, Doctor?" Patrick asked.

"He's doing much better now, resting comfortably. Mrs. McCormick, we're putting your husband through a cardiac workup, but so far it's negative. I believe he may have had a panic attack, but we need to finish testing."

"What?" Patrick and his mother said at the same time. His mom gasped and his own mouth dropped open. His dad didn't panic.

The doctor nodded. "Panic attack symptoms sometimes mimic cardiac issues."

She shook her head.

"My dad doesn't—he's never panicked." Patrick answered for her. *This is unreal. Dad and anxiety?*

"The testing will take several hours and we'll possibly keep him overnight as well. Please, get something to eat while you wait. We have a cafeteria downstairs."

"I'll eat later," his mom said. "I'd like to see him now."

The doctor nodded and Patrick's mom left with her.

Sandy sat down next to him.

Numb from worry first and then relief, Patrick propped his elbows on his knees. Sandy placed a hand over his.

"If you want to see him, you probably can." Sandy's voice dipped low like he didn't want to disturb him.

"I don't think so. Not yet. I'm still processing."

"That's okay, too." Sandy squeezed his hands. "How do you think your mom is doing?"

Patrick could only imagine. She must be worried, of course, and in as much shock as he was. He didn't know what it was like to have the person you love in the hospital. He hoped his dad would be less stubborn than usual and more open to the idea of slowing down. "Maybe we should get Dad some pajamas?" His mind circled in a tangle of thoughts.

"We can, or we can wait and see if they're going to keep him overnight."

Patrick nodded. *What would I have done without Sandy today? He shines brighter than the star on a Christmas tree. He gives me hope.* His heart picked up speed. "That's a better idea."

Sandy turned to a side table, sorting through magazines. "Do you want to read one of these?"

Dad's in the hospital. If I learn anything about today is that life is short. How often does a guy like Sandy come to Mayfield? You're his boss. Please tell me we can figure this out. "Will you go out on a date with me?"

Sandy's mouth dropped opened and the magazines fell out of his hand. "What?"

If the abrupt question surprised Sandy, Patrick was amazed by it. He couldn't believe he'd asked, but now that the question was out there, it felt right. He slid his fingers around Sandy's wrist in a smooth move he hoped was both gentle and genuine. "I'm your boss, so you can say no and I guarantee no repercussions. No pressure—"

Luckily, Sandy seemed unconcerned about that. His face lit up with pure joy. "A hundred times yes!"

He couldn't stop the smile from stretching across his mouth. He relaxed back in his chair, pleased that something good happened.

"Were you seriously worried I'd say no?" Sandy angled

his body toward Patrick.

"About this much." He held up his thumb and forefinger squished together.

Sandy nudged him playfully in the shoulder.

Colleen returned from visiting dad. "He looks pale." She took a seat beside him.

"Should we get something to eat?" Sandy asked, leaning forward to make eye contact with her.

"I'm not sure I'm hungry."

Sandy stood and held his hand out to her. "Let's go, and maybe if you see something you like then your stomach will catch up."

A crooked smile appeared on her face.

As they rode the elevator down, Patrick leaned close to Sandy. "You're great with my parents."

"I haven't met any others. I'm honored that yours are the first. Although, how can they not love me? I'm funny, I know a ridiculous amount about pop culture, and my manners are impeccable except when I'm eating ramen. But who can slurp noodles without making a mess? Actually, I take that back. You've seen me eat, so it's no use lying that I'm like a polar bear taking out a seal."

Patrick didn't realize how much he needed that stress breaker until his shoulders lowered, relaxing.

After they finished having dinner, they made their way back to the emergency bay. Patrick yawned as he flipped through an old copy of *Sports Illustrated*, while his dad slept. His mom hummed as she worked on a crossword puzzle with Sandy, who was only slightly better at it than she was.

Dr. Gupta pushed back the curtain. "His room is ready, so tonight all of you need to go home. We'll talk more tomorrow. Do you have any questions for me?"

His mom shook her head.

"See you tomorrow." The doctor gave a wave and was gone.

"Do you want to say goodbye before we head out?" Patrick asked, knowing she would want a moment with dad before leaving.

"I'll go get the truck warmed up and meet you out front?" Sandy glanced between Patrick and his mom.

"Thanks."

Since his dad was already fast asleep the goodbye was quick. They collected their coats from the rack, slipping them on as they moved. Through the lobby windows, they could see that Sandy had parked the SUV close to the front sliding doors.

Once they were inside the vehicle, his mom patted Sandy on the shoulder. "Thank you, Honey, for being here tonight. You are truly one of a kind."

Sandy's eyebrows bounced. "Hear that?"

Patrick ran a hand over his face. *He's too much. And I like it.*

———

As carefully as possible, Sandy drove them to Patrick's home. Normally, he drove almost as fast as his friend stock car driver Bobbi Yoshida-Barnes trying to win at Daytona, but the day had been hectic enough without risking a five-car pileup on these icy roads.

Patrick slipped his phone out of his thumbs started flying over a text. "Checking in with the stores. Mom, do you have Eric's phone number? I need to make certain everything's okay in Madison and tell him he'll need to manage the store for an undetermined time."

Colleen handed her phone to Patrick.

Sandy didn't want to leave Patrick and Colleen alone tomorrow, but helping out at the store might be more useful. If they needed him, he'd be there for them in a heartbeat. *Okay, maybe I'm still reeling from the fact that he asked me out. This incredibly cute man wants to spend time with me.* "Do you want me to come with you to the hospital tomorrow?"

Patrick's phone vibrated. He read the text then said to Sandy, "Chelsea will handle the store. I think you should join them. There's the stuff for the site, the funding page, and I need Chelsea to play Santa, so you'll have to balance in between that for a couple of hours." He rested his eyes and settled into the head rest.

Sandy turned into Patrick's drive. "No problem."

Patrick's phone vibrated again. Slowly, he scanned the text. "Eric said to keep him posted on Dad and not to worry about the store."

As they exited the SUV, the evening caught up with all of them as they practically crawled to the front door. It looked to Sandy as if they were all traveling in slow motion. Once the front door swung open, Moonshine darted to the front tree.

"Oh shit, I totally forgot her. She's really going to hate me now," Sandy said as the dog ran around the yard, bouncing through the snow.

Patrick held the door for Colleen. "Don't worry. Chels fed her and took her out for a walk this afternoon. She was at the store most of the day. Evidently, they made her a name tag, so now she's an official employee."

"If she gets paid more than I do then I want an opportunity to renegotiate."

"You're saying you'd accept kibble as payment?"

Sandy rolled his eyes, and Moonshine came running up to Patrick, wagging her tail. "Okay, yeah, I see how it is now."

Patrick scratched behind Moonshine's ears.

Sandy entered the house and started removing his outer layers.

Colleen hugged Patrick and then Sandy. "Good night boys and thank you for . . . " Overwhelmed with emotions, her words trailed off, and then she waved a hand as she retired to the bedroom.

Untying his boots, Sandy glanced up at Patrick. "Will she be alright?"

Patrick dried off Moonshine and then started to remove his jacket. "I think so. We've never had a scare like this. The stress from the store, and not exercising have taken their toll on Dad."

Sandy could understand. He couldn't fathom how he'd react if his mom ever got sick or Julia. It was sad to think he only had two people he loved that much. Sandy walked into the kitchen. "I know it's late, but I'm going to make hot cocoa. Any interest?"

Behind him, Patrick's padded feet followed. "Yeah, I could use a comfort drink tonight." He grabbed the milk from the refrigerator, then a pan and some cocoa.

Sandy fired up the stove and started his hot chocolate process. Most of the time his mouth got away from him, but he had to ask about Patrick's missing sibling. "Um, so are you planning on texting your criminal brother about your dad?"

Leaning against the counter, Patrick looked weary. "Am I a terrible person for not thinking of him?"

Shrugging, Sandy stirred the milk. "Ha! Not in my book."

Dropping his head, Patrick's features twisted in thought. "Mom would really like to see Dolan, especially this time of the year and with Dad . . . "

"Will your dad be okay if opens his eyes to see . . . Dolan, was it?" Irish and Scottish names were so unusual. Dolan sounded like a foghorn to Sandy.

Patrick handed the cocoa mix to Sandy. "I'd say we wait on springing Dolan on Dad, but Mom might have other ideas."

"Call me crazy, but that sounds ominous."

From a cupboard, Patrick retrieved mugs and scooted them near the stove. "He's the baby."

Sandy flipped off the stove. "Pfft, that's ridiculous."

With a disbelieving look on his face, Patrick leaned a hand against the counter and moved into Sandy's personal space.

"Don't give me that look. Yes, I'm an only child, so I have no idea what the hell you're talking about."

"Yup, I knew it."

Pouring the liquid, Sandy relished Patrick's invasion of his space. *I'm pretty certain it's not the hot cocoa that's warming me up.* He couldn't keep his heart from doing backflips nor did he want to. "I'm gonna need you to elaborate on that."

"You have an independent spirit, you want to help people, and you're ambitious."

He slid a mug over to Patrick and shrugged. "These things can be said about a lot of people, and not all of them are only children."

Patrick guided them to the living room couch. "Fair enough." Patrick sat at one end of the leather couch and slid a couple of pillows behind his back.

Sandy took a seat opposite him. "Wow, this couch is cold. Why did you buy this thing?"

Patrick grunted. "My ex. Wasn't the worst thing he talked me into. I might still have a time share in Florida if it wasn't taken out by the hurricane."

Sandy tossed a blanket from the back of the couch over his out-stretched legs. "Sounds horrible. Glad to know I'm not the only one who has terrible taste in men." He tapped Patrick's knee. "Hey, no sense freezing."

Patrick threw his legs up on the other side of Sandy's, and they shared the blanket.

"Do you know where Dolan is?" Sandy sipped his cocoa. The closeness of Patrick made him turn gooey and warm inside. Having a pair of strong well-muscled legs pressed against his made him want to forgo the talking and jump to the making out part.

But Patrick shook his head, and a crease formed between his eyes. Clearly, his thoughts were still elsewhere.

"How do you feel about him?"

Puffing his cheeks out, Patrick ran a hand through his hair. "Angry. Worried. Sad. And it's so annoying to miss him, but I do. He's funny and he's smart even though he never applied himself at school—which was so irritating. Most of the time I don't know if I want to put him in a half nelson or hug him."

Sandy stretched an arm against the back of the couch. He could listen to the soothing timbre of Patrick's voice all night long. Being blissed out on his guy was absurd since they didn't really know one another, but damn if it didn't feel like they did.

Patrick leaned forward and squeezed Sandy's foot. "What's with the look?"

Sandy covered his face with both hands. He wasn't prepared, yet, to confess embarrassing thoughts with him.

And then Patrick crawled over the blanket, and Sandy dropped his hands. Leaning in, Patrick's mouth hovered a scant breath away from his. He inhaled the delicious chocolate scent mixed with pine body wash, providing him with a heady aroma as irresistible as a Christmas morning. Those green eyes stared him down. *Gah, you better kiss me now you frickin' handsome-assed Santa.* Entranced by Patrick's pink lips, Sandy couldn't take it anymore. He reached up with both hands and pulled him into a kiss. The small grunt Patrick released tickled Sandy to no end. He kicked his way free of the blanket and wrapped his legs around the fit man, bringing him tightly against his hips.

Patrick's body relaxed into Sandy. The weight of Patrick against him made everything brighter. He sneaked his hands underneath the waistband of Patrick's jeans and boxers. Excited to finally get some skin-on-skin contact, he grabbed Patrick's ass. *His butt is as cut as the rest of him!*

Patrick was the first to break away. He smiled while trying to catch his breath. "I really enjoyed that."

"Same." Sandy moved his hands up from Patrick's tight butt to his sinewy back. "My hands may have gotten away from me."

"I liked it, but . . . "

His scrambled brain strained to come up with a reason for Patrick's abrupt end to their make-out session. "Right. Your mom's here."

Patrick snickered into his arm. "I never got busted making out with anyone when I was young."

"If this is a challenge, I'd be totally game to see how long I can give you a blow job before she catches us."

Patrick's features turned a blazing red.

"You were totally thinking that, too. Right?" Sandy said, razzing Patrick.

Patrick dropped his head into Sandy's shoulder. He inhaled and exhaled. His breath tickled.

"Fine. We won't horrify your mother." He ran his fingers through Patrick's hair, toying with the ends by his neck.

"If you keep that up, I'm going to fall asleep on you."

"We could continue this in your bedroom."

Patrick shook his head. "Thin walls. When we do have sex, I don't want either of us to hold back."

Sandy debated stopping the combing. Patrick was really heavy in that solid, muscle man kind of way, but he liked it. He liked having this thick man weigh him down. *I could get used to this kind of thing.*

CHAPTER 10

Patrick kissed Sandy behind his ear. The adorable man wiggled and let out a giggle too. He rubbed his beard against Sandy's neck, and he was pretty certain that was something he liked a lot since he was clinging to Patrick with all his might. Patrick popped up on his arms, hovering above Sandy. He gave him a quick peck on the lips and then hopped off him. He held his hand out. "Let's go. We'll have time to play reindeer games some other time." He pulled Sandy up from the couch.

"That's so not what we call sexy times nowadays."

Exhaustion hit him as Patrick pulled Sandy by the hand toward his bedroom. It'd be a miracle if they did more than sleep tonight. He'd only known him two days, and it was too soon, After all, he'd asked Sandy on a date. And they deserved a date. They deserved romance and dancing and laughing at stupid jokes. "I never claimed to be a cool kid."

"Yeah, Honey, I know. Your wardrobe consists of more flannel and boots than a Pacific Northwest lesbian."

Patrick beamed at that. He did love flannel.

Once they were in the bedroom, he took off his shirt and tossed it on the bed, exchanging it for his flannel pajama top. "Yeah, but I think you kind of like me in it. You can't take your eyes off me when I put it on."

"Oh, I'm soooo not checking out the flannel. Have you seen yourself?" A set of mischievous eyes scanned Patrick up and down like he was the last Christmas cookie on a plate.

Patrick looked down at his chest and abs as he buttoned. He was by no means ripped with a ton of muscles, but he was athletic. Although now that his dad was in the hospital with anxiety issues, maybe it was time to rethink his mental health habits.

"What's with the frowny face?" Sandy moved close and placed his hands on his shoulders.

"I hate putting so much responsibility on Chels and you. Maybe I should go into the store tomorrow."

Sandy shook his head. "Not a chance. Your parents need you, and my friend Julia was fanfuckingtastic at avoiding a lot of tough family stuff and that's the same kind of excuse she used to make. I don't think you're like her and all avoid-y. Do what you need to do. We can handle it."

Patrick planted a chaste kiss on Sandy's cheek. He couldn't help worrying about everything right now. *What would happen if Dad died? Does he even have a will? I need to check in with Mom tomorrow and find out what kind of plans they've made for the future.*

———

The next morning Patrick and his mom dropped Sandy off at the store. He was kind of grateful to be going into work instead of going to a hospital. He wasn't afraid of medical facilities; it's that they weren't his altogether favorite place to be, especially on any day ending in a y. Although, he was warming up to them since Patrick asked him out inside of one.

As Sandy climbed the stairs to the second floor, he wondered if Patrick only asked him out because he was panicking about his father's condition. He didn't want to think that, but his brain was playing all sorts of games with him. Specifically, the "you're-not-good-enough-for-him" game. The worst self-esteem game of all time.

He pushed into the locker room muttering his personal version of an affirmation. "You are cute. You are funny. You are funfuckingfantastic—and screw him if he can't see that." When Sandy glanced up, he came face-to-face with Chelsea, who didn't even blink at his verbal diatribe.

Chelsea stood there in the Santa costume. The sleeves and pants were short on them as if the entire suit were washed in hot water and then shrunk some more in a high heat dryer. Sandy covered his mouth, holding in his smile and laughter. *Man, I thought I had problems.*

"Don't you dare."

Sandy held his hands in the air, surrendering. Costume issues weren't on his list of problems or things to do, but he was creative enough to figure something out. "I have an idea.

Come with me." He led them to the men's department where he scrounged around for an extra-extra-extra-large red flannel shirt. "It should be long enough, and we can do the suspenders over the shirt and padded belly. If there's a sewing kit around here, then I can rip the fake fur off the jacket and pants."

"You can sew?"

Sandy placed a hand on his chest. "Honey, I am a master of many talents."

Chelsea shed the red jacket and slipped into the shirt. "What about these pants? I can barely walk in them. If I sit, they'll split open."

Sandy headed for a stack of clearance jeans. "How about a hipster Santa?" He grabbed a pair of tall and wide pants and eye-balled them against Chelsea.

They took the jeans off the hanger. "Hipster. Worst word in the history of words. But it'll do." They slipped off the red pants, revealing a pair of long underwear.

Sandy raised a brow. "Those are hideous."

"Don't knock 'em until you try 'em. It gets cold in this store." Chelsea tucked the shirt in and fastened the suspenders. They turned around for Sandy.

He scrutinized the costume changes. "Once you get the boots on and everything else, I think you'll pull it off." Sandy glanced at his cell. "What time do we start the photo session this morning?"

"Nine until noon. We probably won't have many."

Sandy started to move in the direction of the locker room. "I need to change into my adorable elf uniform, and then I'll have to sew everything like a mad man."

"And I'll get the store open. We only have two other employees on the floor."

Sandy nodded as they went their separate ways.

———

Two hours and only three photo ops later, Sandy and Chelsea stood in the curtained area. Chelsea printed out the photos that were ordered by a handful of families online while Sandy prepared the matting and framing.

"I'd like to ask you a random question, but I know how you hate gossiping . . . " Sandy slid the clips closed on the back of a frame.

"Ask me whatever since I'm positive you're like a chipmunk."

Sandy placed a hand on a hip, staring them down.

"You're going to keep digging until there's a mess," Chelsea snarked.

He threw a hand in the air. "Puhlease, terrible comparison. If anything, I'm an adorable prairie dog."

They rolled their eyes at him.

"Whatever." Sandy began to cut the next matte. "Have you met Dolan?"

"Oh, he's told you about his brother?" A half-smile graced Chelsea's features as if pleased that Patrick had shared that much with Sandy. "Dolan's a wildcard."

"If he came into town, then it would be a bad thing?" Sandy tapped his blade against the tabletop, considering the chaos Dolan's arrival could create.

"Hey, I could be off base. The guy could have changed."

He returned to his cutting. "Do you have any siblings?"

"Two sisters."

"Funny, I wouldn't have guessed."

"Me neither." Chelsea moved around Sandy and started the boxing and wrapping process. "One in Seattle and the other in D.C."

"Where do you fall in the order of things?"

"At the bottom."

Sandy snorted. "How's that now?"

They sighed at his antics. "Youngest. But the other two are clueless when it comes to caretaking."

He handed over another framed set. "Is your mom, well, how is she?"

Chelsea gave a half-shrug as they focused on measuring and tearing Christmas wrapping off a roll. "Struggling. It might be a miracle if she makes it through the new year. I'm glad I'm with her, but I feel guilty for not being with her all the years she wasn't sick."

"I would tell you to not feel that way, but it's been my experience that when people say that to me, I just want to smack them."

"I can relate." Chelsea folded the paper around the photo box.

Sandy stood up and bent over backward, stretching his back. "BTW, I need to steal you away this afternoon for some marketing stuff." He bounced his brows, hoping they'd be a good sport for the video promos.

"The feeling of running in the opposite direction is so

strong right now."

Somehow, he knew it'd take more convincing on his part to get them onboard. "Can you be bribed?"

"Perhaps."

Sandy rubbed his hands together like Scrooge screwing a kid out of some change. He knew exactly what he was gonna get them.

"And now it's deep regret," they said as they slapped a piece of tape on a package.

Together they completed the boxing and wrapping of the rest of the photos. Once that was finished, they resumed their photo duties. While Sandy adjusted the tripod, a haggard forty-something man bumped into a rotating stand of ski goggles. Sandy ran over and caught the stand and some of the merchandise before everything went flying. He planted it back upright and then turned, almost running into the unsteady man.

"You have my job," the obviously drunk fellow slurred. He reeked of a malt beverage.

"I'm not following," Sandy said, trying to step back, but unfortunately the drunk stepped into his personal space and tried to poke him in the chest. Since the stranger was so out of it, he only managed to fall forward. Chelsea swooped in out of nowhere and caught him.

"Wayne, why are you here? Leave or I'm calling the cops." They held the drunk up by the elbow and back. Sandy grabbed hold of him on the other side.

"I deserve. I deserve to work." Wayne stumbled over his own feet, but Chelsea steadied him.

"You need help. Did you drive?" they asked.

"Mmm, nope. I can't find my car."

Chelsea sighed. They searched the jacket pocket nearest them. "Check the other," they said to Sandy when they found nothing.

Sandy pulled out a set of keys and handed them to Chelsea. They stuffed the keys in their pants pocket.

"Maybe he could sleep it off in the locker room?" Sandy didn't know what the process was for having a disruptive inebriated person roaming around the store. The only way he knew to keep everyone safe was to keep him under a watchful eye.

"You took my job," Wayne repeated to Sandy.

Sandy shot Chelsea a what-the-hell-is-he-talking-about look over the top of Wayne's head.

"Fired the day you were hired," they mumbled. "Yeah, let's take him there." Chelsea led them to the elevator. "If you get sick in the elevator, you're cleaning it up, Wayne. Do you hear me?"

Wayne laughed hysterically as if he thought the entire situation was a big joke.

"Should we text Patrick about this?" Sandy asked as they deposited Wayne on the staff couch. "It might be wise to let him know that an irrational ex-employee showed up out of the blue."

They walked toward the stairs. "I'll text him and fill out an incident report."

"Do you think this Wayne guy is dangerous?"

Chelsea shook their head. "He's a puppy. The only one

he'll probably hurt someday is himself."

"Unless he drives while under the influence."

They held up Wayne's keys. "I'll call Sheriff Gómez and let him know the situation." Chelsea rounded the corner at one of the unused registers. They unlocked a drawer and dropped Wayne's keys away, locking them up safely.

Sandy glanced out at the big flakes falling outside. "Do you think we'll get anyone for our last Santa hour?"

They followed his gaze and shrugged.

"I'm going to grab Patrick's laptop. I can work on a couple of things down here as we wait." Sandy said.

Chelsea leaned back against the counter. "I hope you can save the store. I'd miss being here every day."

If he could help save it, he would. Sandy moved toward the stairs. Chelsea admitting that they were invested in the store and Patrick was a big deal. He got the sense that they didn't open up very often and perhaps even had some social anxiety issues. As he opened the door to the office, his phone buzzed from his back pocket. He slipped it out of his elf costume pants and checked the messages.

> Dad looks better today. Thinking of you . . .

> Miss you, too. ;)

> What are you wearing? LOL

> Something only someone very bad would wear . . . bells on shoes

Hot

Did you text your bro?

Mom did.

And . . . ?

He's on his way. Doctor is here. Talk later.

That wasn't abrupt, right? No, he had to go because the doctor arrived. It's your imagination running away from you and not Patrick running away from you. Although, I wouldn't blame him. Ugh, shut up voice! Sandy grabbed the laptop and returned downstairs. From outside sleet beat against the windows. Unfortunately, the change in weather would only hurt the store. Snow was a common part of winter in northern Illinois, but sleet and freezing temperatures were another.

He dashed off a text to Patrick alerting him to check the weather. If he and Chelsea got stuck at the store, that'd be one thing, but Colleen and Patrick being stuck at the hospital would guarantee a sleepless night with all the noise. Then Sandy flipped open the laptop and started tweaking the website.

———

At a hospital vending machine, Patrick jammed a thumb into the button for a granola bar. His mind was still blown that his mom had called freaking Dolan. But what really got him was that Dolan had lived in Chicago all this time. He wasn't in Florida or New York or any other criminal playground where Patrick thought a criminal would prosper. As far as humans go, his brother sucked. Of course, his mom had known where Dolan was the entire time, and of course she'd hidden the information from him and his dad. She'd always protected and coddled Dolan to the point of excess. Grown adults paid consequences for their bad actions, but his mom didn't think it was fair to outright banish him from the family and not communicate with him. She said Dolan was working in sales now for a big, hoity-toity company. Knowing Dolan, he was probably scamming money out of the elderly or making children work in a sweatshop. The fact that his mom believed Dolan's malarkey proved she was oblivious to his conniving ways.

Patrick bit into the granola bar and chewed. It was stale. *That figures.* He pitched the entire thing into the trash.

His mom came up next to him and hit a few buttons. Two packs of peanuts dropped down, and she handed one to Patrick. "These might be better."

He ripped open the package. "I can't believe you knew where he was this entire time."

"If I'd told you, then you would've made a fuss—like you're doing now." She popped a couple of peanuts into her mouth.

"He's a criminal." Despite his best efforts, heat crept up his neck. He didn't want to argue with his mom, but he couldn't remain silent. "He stole from the store. When he was confronted, he got physical with Dad and pushed him."

"Ack, things became heated." She waved away Dolan's mistakes like he'd merely left milk out on the counter. "Tempers run high in this family."

"If I hadn't stepped in when he was fighting with Dad, who knows if he would have stopped." Patrick threw his arms in the air as frustration surged in his veins. "How can you trust him? How can any of us?"

"He needed time to figure out his life. Not everyone follows one path at all times."

Patrick didn't understand what the hell that meant. "I get that we all hit a bump in the road, but he's a criminal. Technically, he should be in jail. But somehow you talked Dad into letting it all slide, and the bastard walked away and left us to clean up his mess."

"It was all an accident."

Shocked, Patrick's jaw went slack. "Ordering a hamburger and getting a cheeseburger is an accident. Slipping on an icy sidewalk. Putting on two different socks. But what he did wasn't an accident. It was purposeful."

Colleen tossed her empty package in the bin. "He was trying to live up to too high of expectations."

Patrick gritted his teeth. *That's a bunch of bullshit.* "He never applied himself to anything except robbing us blind, and, wow, did he ever fucking exceed my expectations when he did that."

"Don't swear." Colleen placed one hand over the other. She fell silent as a nurse passed by. "I don't want you upsetting your father. Go outside and get some air."

His nostrils flared. There was only so much mothering he could take. "If he's so wonderful, why hasn't he been around?" Patrick's hands clenched in anger. "I'll tell you why, he's waiting. Waiting for you to convince Dad and me to forgive him and forget. You know what? That isn't going to happen. Ever."

Colleen placed a hand on his shoulder. "You don't mean that."

He nodded, trying to get his breathing under control.

"It's Christmastime. Your family needs you."

"I've been here. I'm always here." Patrick stormed toward the nearest exit.

As he ran to the hospital's main entrance, his ears started to ring. When he shoved the door handle leading outside, a cool blast of air hit him in the face. He took a deep breath, allowing the wintery breeze and sloppy sleet to pelt him in the face and reduce his body heat.

Marching down the sidewalk, he huffed. Dolan wasn't what he wanted to be worried about. He wished he could be thinking about what to wear on his date with Sandy or picking out a restaurant—anything but his nefarious, scum-sucking brother. It was sheer bad timing that he was getting involved with a guy he liked just as his job and family were blowing up.

He should have taken the phone from his mom when he had the chance. He could've prevented a visit from Dolan if only he'd been bold enough to say no. No, you can't come visit. No, we can't forgive you. No, I don't want to see you ever again. But Patrick hadn't said any of that.

He'd allowed his mom to talk to Dolan. She laughed with him and practically cooed over his every word. Patrick's blood boiled seeing her this fooled, but he couldn't break her bubble of happiness, especially while her husband slept in the hospital room. But it wasn't fair. His brother would use their father's condition as an opportunity to return and take advantage of the situation, and Patrick couldn't stop it.

"Fuck!" Patrick kicked a pile of slush. He stopped walking and placed his hands on his hips. His phone buzzed from his jacket pocket. Sandy's photo popped up. He hit the FaceTime icon and gave him a wave.

"Whoever pissed you off has a lot of explaining to do," Sandy said.

"You can tell?" He tried to relax his features, but he was still too wound up.

"Ah yeah, you look like you're ready to kick a reindeer."

Just Sandy's presence on the screen made the tension in Patrick's shoulders loosen. "I'm happy to see your face."

Sandy tilted his head. A shade of pink colored his cheeks. "Missing yours, too. This might cheer you up: I managed to incorporate the website changes annnd I got Chelsea on TikTok."

Patrick couldn't stop the laugh from blurting out.

CHAPTER 11

nside his dad's hospital room, Patrick stuffed his earbuds in and hit the first McCormick's General Store TikTok. On screen, Chelsea stood in the kitchen supplies section of the store. They picked up a Scottish spurtle and did a hilarious two-minute commentary on what they thought the thing was and why everyone should have one. Sandy's genius plan, which included three other videos for today, was getting them noticed on the app and fast. They already had over ten thousand likes on that first TikTok. It seemed likely that Chelsea and the store could be a big hit if these numbers kept up.

His mother patted him on the knee and wagged her hand for him to follow her out into the corridor.

Patrick tucked away his earbuds and slipped his phone into his back pocket, but stopped short at the sight of his wayward brother standing next to mom. He stood there staring at his brother's familiar face, but the suit, the tie, and the inappropriate fancy shoes threw him off. *Loafers in Illinois winter weather? What the hell is wrong with him?* The clean-shaven face and perfectly styled hair didn't deceive Patrick for a minute.

Dolan took a step forward, extending his hand.

Patrick looked down at the cheating, lying man's hand.

"Go on then," Colleen encouraged.

Patrick slapped his palm into Dolan's and squeezed.

"Yeesh, that's still a grip you got there, Bro."

That's right I do, asshole.

Dolan ripped his hand out of Patrick's grasp. Sure, it was petty, but Dolan deserved way more pain and suffering than that. "Mom said you have a job."

Dolan unfolded and refolded his cashmere jacket over his arm. "I'm vice president at Massive Bank & Loan."

That sounds completely made up. "Do you have a card?"

His brother stared and then threw him a slimy smile. "Of course." He reached into his jacket pocket and slid a card from an engraved case. Dolan held it out to Patrick.

He snatched the little cardboard square. *Anyone with a printer can do this.* "How about your bank identification?"

Mom gasped as if Patrick revealed that Santa wasn't real to all the kids in the Peds Unit.

"It's fine." Dolan rubbed her back. He exchanged the cards for his billfold then flipped it open and took out a MB&L ID card.

With doubtful eyes, Patrick inspected the photo, the name, the employee ID number. He couldn't believe it. *What idiot would hire him as a vice president at their bank?* Although, Dolan didn't have a criminal record, so naturally they wouldn't know what kind of deceitful and corrupt character they'd hired.

"Tell him the good news," Mom encouraged Dolan.

There's more? Patrick thought he might gag. How much am I supposed to believe here?

Dolan put his things into his suit jacket. "I'm engaged."

Patrick gaped in disbelief. *What poor sap of a woman would be desperate and stupid enough to fall for his wonderland of lies?*

"Well, congratulate him," Mom instructed Patrick. "Go on."

"Congrats. Who's the lucky gal?"

"Emily. She works out of our London offices. Very posh as they say in the UK."

"That sounds so fancy." Mom beamed.

Get me a bucket.

Without making eye contact, Dolan nodded at the hospital room behind Patrick. "Is Dad awake?"

"Off and on."

His brother took a step forward toward the room, but Patrick placed a hand on his chest, preventing him from moving further. "Listen, we haven't told him you're here, and frankly, I think this is a horrible idea. If you so much as say one thing to upset him or alter his blood pressure, I will toss you out the door so fucking fast your head will spin."

"Patrick, language." Mom glanced around the corridor almost in fear that a passerby would overhear Patrick cursing. As if using bad words in public was the biggest problem they had to deal with.

"I understand where you're coming from. I messed up. In honor of the holiday season, I'm hoping all of us can open our hearts and forgive one another," Dolan said with a smarmy smirk.

That was the biggest load of reindeer crap I've ever heard. He's lucky Mom is here or I'd punch that disgusting look off his face. "Stay put. We'll let him know you're here. If he doesn't want to see you, then that'll be that." Patrick spun around with Colleen following him.

The scent of coffee hung in the air, greeting Patrick and his mom. His dad was on the bed with his eyes closed, but he could tell his dad wasn't asleep as the muscle in his jaw jumped.

Mom rubbed his shoulder until his father opened his eyes. She kissed his cheek.

He squeezed his dad's warm hand. "How are you feeling?"

The old man grunted.

"Are you up for some company?" Mom ran her fingers over his hair.

"Not long," Dad said as he shifted in the bed as if seeking a comfortable position.

"It's Dolan, Dad." Dolan stepped into the room, tossing his expensive jacket on a chair. He moved to the bed.

"You didn't wait for me to come get you." Patrick gritted his teeth. If he cracked a molar, he'd send Dolan the bill.

"Why not rip the Band-Aid off?"

"Boys," Mom pleaded.

"Can't believe you're here." Dad's eyes opened wide as if surprised to see his youngest. "Glad you're here son."

"Me, too, Dad. I love you."

The thought of throwing Dolan out the window crossed Patrick's mind. He couldn't believe what his dad just said. After all the years of listening to him bitch and moan about Dolan screwing over the family and the store, and how much of an impact the money loss had on their stores, it was inconceivable that he would welcome Dolan with open arms. *Whatever they're feeding him in the IV must promote memory loss and kindness.* He gripped the bed rail until his fists turned white.

"I knew he'd be elated to see you. Now we have the family back for Christmas. Such a blessing." Colleen squeezed Dolan into her side.

"I need to check in on the store." Patrick shrugged into his jacket and moved toward the door.

"You're driving there? Now?" Mom's features twisted with disappointment.

"You've got Dolan. I'll return before visiting hours end to say goodnight to Dad."

————

Business at the store picked up for a while in the afternoon and then went quiet. Sandy was supposedly helping Chelsea with inventory, but he was actually scrolling on his phone for restaurants around Mayfield.

"There's got to be at least one fancy schmancy restaurant in the vicinity of this town. Any ideas?"

Chelsea shifted boxes of tube socks on a shelf. "Chicago?"

He looked at them, wondering if they were joking. "Maybe I should cook for him instead."

"Can you?" Chelsea wrote on the clipboard.

"Mostly experiments."

They released a heavy sigh as they tapped their pen against the board. "I can't believe I'm going to say this, but I know of a really good chef in town."

He leapt off his chair. "Gurl, don't be holding out on me now. Spill."

"You met her the other night at Ace's: Sam."

He deflated. Sandy wanted something special and not hamburgers or sandwiches. "Ah, I was kinda going for something more *Top Chef* and less roadhouse roadkill."

They pursed their lips at his assumption. "She went to culinary school."

"To learn how to make chili?"

"You're being a dick. Sam is probably a better chef than one of those Michelin starred restaurant chefs in the city. She studied in Paris."

Shocked, he stood there with a gaping mouth, frozen like the North Pole.

"And before you say something snarky like, why is she living here, it's because she likes it here."

He folded his arms. *Yes, I was totally going to say that.* "I would never."

Chelsea shot him what he was coming to know as their deadpan stare.

"Fine, you got me." Throwing his arms in the air, he needed their help with Sam, so he conceded defeat. "Do you think she'd be interested? I'd pay, of course. I need a venue besides his house."

Chelsea bobbed their head. "Have it here."

Sandy glanced around the storage room. This was not a conducive room for a romantic dinner for two.

"Not *here*, here, but the second level. Put up a table, nice linen, dim the overhead lights, turn on the Christmas tree lights . . . "

It hit Sandy that if he got Chelsea to help Sam then maybe he could nudge those two together. "Would you be free to lend me a hand with set-up and serving? I'd pay you, too."

Chelsea shifted their weight from one leg to the other. "I'd have to have the night nurse stay longer, but I think I could swing it."

"Do you think we could do this tonight? I'd love to surprise him."

"You're fucking serious?" Exhaling a loud breath, Chelsea set their clipboard and pen to the side. They reached in their back pocket and started texting.

I think I have one decent shirt for dinner. This is cray exciting. Whoo-hoo! His cheeks hurt from the giant smile on his face.

Chelsea's phone dinged several times. "Sam is in. Do you want to give her ideas or tell her to be creative?" The phone dinged a few more times. Obviously, Sam had a lot to say.

"Allergies? Forget this—take my phone and answer her." Chelsea tossed their cell to Sandy, who completely missed it.

"I don't do sports," he said when Chelsea slapped a palm over their eyes. Sandy scooped the phone off the floor and began chatting with Sam, whose giddiness at the idea of a private dinner equaled his. He chewed on the side of his thumb as his nerves started to get the best of him.

Sandy stepped over to Chelsea and returned their phone. "All set. Now what about the ambiance?"

Chelsea gave him a quick head nod as if pointing to follow them. They led the way to a storage room on the second floor where odds and ends of office supplies and furniture landed. A square table with two chairs on top of it stood in the corner.

"That'll do. And a tablecloth or something to make it look less business professional?"

Chelsea stood there for a moment. They scratched their nose and then snapped their fingers. They were on the move. Sandy jogged to catch up. They entered Patrick's office and headed to the closet. "These might look familiar." They pulled down a set of Christmas paper tablecloths, the same ones they used during the kickoff celebration.

"If the food is as amazing as you think it's going to be, then hopefully that'll distract both of us from noticing the dancing Santas and reindeer below our plates." He couldn't believe he was going to have a first date dinner on holiday table decoration.

"I say lean into it since we have matching paper plates and napkins to go with it." Chelsea held up one of each.

He tapped a finger against his lips. If they dimmed the lights low enough, then maybe Sandy could forget everything else. This was starting to look more like a child's birthday party than a sexy meal. *Remember this is Patrick. He doesn't need china patterns or whatevs.* Sandy considered Patrick. *He likes flannel. He likes plaid. He walks to work.* "Maybe it's kind of perfect?"

"Super. Now can I please go back to counting stock?" Chelsea pushed the napkins and plates into Sandy's chest as they walked away.

Sandy couldn't explain it, but when he looked at the dancing Santas all he could see was Patrick in his Santa suit doing a happy dance.

———

Patrick was in such a funk when he stormed out of the hospital, he didn't drive to the store. In Chelsea's hands the store was fine. Instead, he drove to the nearest drive-thru and ordered two double cheeseburgers and an extra-large box of fries. He brought them back to the hospital parking lot and sat in his vehicle, eating his emotions, as he stared at the hospital entrance. His phone buzzed from his inside pocket. Sandy's face appeared on the FaceTime. Patrick quickly looked at his own face in the review mirror and dusted crumbs and salt off his beard. He glanced down at his shirt and jacket, crossing his fingers that he hadn't dribbled ketchup on his clothing. Once he looked semi-presentable, he hit the accept button.

"Hi there, handsome stranger." Sandy waved at Patrick.

"Hi, yourself." Patrick mirrored Sandy's smile. *Please tell me that I do not have sesame seeds stuck in my teeth.*

"How's everything going with your dad? Are you in your SUV?"

Patrick glanced over the phone at the hospital. "I needed some fresh air. My brother's getting the best of me."

Sandy frowned. "Wish I could do something for you."

He shook his head, trying not to let his emotions run rampant while they were on the phone. "It is what it is. How's everything going? Those TikToks are awesome."

"Going great." Sandy wiggled at the compliment. "Hey, I kind of was wondering if you had dinner plans?"

Patrick's eyes shifted to the empty fast-food containers. "I don't. I'm gonna try to get Mom to leave a little early and relax at the house. You want to go somewhere?"

"Since everything is nuts for you, I have something planned. You don't have to do anything—just say yes."

Patrick nodded his head. "Yeah, I can do that."

"And it's casual intimate, so wear whatever you're comfortable in."

Patrick eyed the empty bag and glanced back at Sandy. "We're not having burgers, are we?"

"We might be in the sticks, but you should know I'm higher maintenance than ground chuck."

Patrick snorted at that and they hung up.

He sat there for another hour waiting for his brother to leave. As soon as Dolan was in his car, driving out of sight, Patrick got out of his truck. It was petty. He didn't care. The less time he spent with Dolan the better. He needed to preserve and protect his mental health. And his mom would try to force them together, which he could only tolerate for less than a half hour. Patrick didn't know if Dolan planned to return that evening, so he'd say goodnight to his dad and convince his mom to come home early. After this emotional day, they all could use a break. As he entered the hospital, the black cloud that had been smothering him all afternoon started to lift. And it was all Sandy's doing. For the first time that day, he had something to smile about. *I have a date!*

CHAPTER 12

In Ace's kitchen, Sandy stood over Sam's shoulder, inhaling the delicious scent of basil, tomato, and pepper soup. A pan of brownies cooled on a counter. He touched the corner of his mouth, checking for drool.

"Can you get him to stop lurking?" Sam said to Chelsea as she moved to a cutting area and peeled a clove of garlic.

"Hey, give her space," Chelsea said from a stool in the corner.

Indicating surrender, he raised his hands in the air and moved next to Chelsea. "Not too much garlic. I want him to kiss me at the end of the night and maybe more."

"Is he telling me what to do in my kitchen?"

Chelsea glared at Sandy. "Sit down and shut up."

"Sitting." He wiggled into the chair. "So, Sam, you cook, you're—not to objectify you as a woman, but hot AF—how on earth are you single?"

A set of daggers fired from Chelsea's eyes at him.

"You're a nosy one." Sam stirred and turned the heat down on the soup.

"You have no idea . . ."

"Let's get the tapas started." Sam grabbed a wooden board from the middle kitchen station.

Chelsea hopped off their seat and walked into the cooler.

Sam flagged Sandy over to her station. "Patrick and Chelsea are friends. Did they threaten you if you hurt him?" She handed him some olives and a spoon. "Put them in this small dish." She reached up for a travel thermos and poured hot soup into it, screwing the lid on and placing the container in a box with a few other items.

"You know they say so little and yet speak so much." Sandy popped an olive in his mouth.

"Stop. You'll ruin your appetite and my hard work." Sam smacked his hand, admonishing him.

"Wow, you're mean." Sandy rubbed the back of his hand.

"I've been itching to do that since I met him," Chelsea said as they returned from the cooler and placed various cheeses on the counter.

That earned Chelsea a nudge and a flirty wink from Sam. *These two. Maybe I could accidently lock them in the walk-in together?* It was agonizing to watch. *Do Patrick and I have this kind of chemistry? Yeah. Oh yeah, we do.* "What time do we have the toy drive tomorrow?"

"Set up at 8 a.m. Patrick usually helps deliver. We need another body and car."

Sam handed Chelsea a bread knife and baguette. "About this thin." She showed them. "I can help in the afternoon."

Sweet silver bells, it's like I planned this or something. Ho! Ho! Ho! "Fantastic. Okay, now question: tell me the full story of Dolan stealing the money from the store." He was going for casual, but that was about as subtle as Santa falling down a chimney.

"Relentless." Chelsea shook their head.

"I'm tired of tiptoeing around it, so I need someone to give me the hot goss."

Sam handed him a cover for the olives.

"Not it." Chelsea said, passing the obligation to Sam.

"Thanks for that." Sam grabbed two containers from the fridge. "This is savory and this is sweet." She held both in the air to show Sandy and tucked them into the box.

"Spicy?" He always liked to know if there was a chance of burning his tongue out of his mouth prior to sitting down at a table.

Sam waved a hand in the air as if he'd be fine. "Patrick was away on a weekend trip, and Dolan was managing the store on his own. He just took the money and ran."

"That's ice cold. Why'd he do it? Drugs? Gambling debts? Addiction to Home Shopping Network?"

"No one really knows, and he hasn't been back since."

"He wasn't arrested? What happened?"

Sam grabbed some figs and sliced them. "Patrick wanted to call my dad, but the elder McCormick's wouldn't hear of it."

"Her dad's the sheriff," Chelsea supplied.

Understanding, he nodded along. "How much did he get away with from the store?"

"Oh, it wasn't just what they had at the store. He cleaned out all the money they had in the business account at the bank, over $50,000."

Shocked, Sandy stood there with a gaping mouth and sloped shoulders.

"And ever since then Patrick's bent over backward to keep it running—even put in his own money. If he didn't have Chelsea and you, I doubt he would have even left the store long enough to visit his dad in the hospital. We're talking about a guy who's living and only living to manage that place." She placed the figs in a container. "I think you're good for him. I can already see that he's beginning to trust at least a couple of people again."

Sandy plastered a smile on his face, but inside he was panicking. *Am I ready for this? What if I fail him like his brother did? Oh shit, I think I've made a huge mistake. Yes, Patrick's a great guy, and except for my best friend Julia, I've never had a long-term or stable relationship in my life. None of my hookups extended into emotions and investment. And now along comes this wonderful guy I barely know, who I'm deceiving about my new job, and I'm going to screw this up.* Discouraged, Sandy picked up a pan of brownies and stuffed one in his mouth. *Beyond delicious! Maybe I should have another one. Or two.*

———

After bringing his mom home, Patrick stood in front of his bedroom mirror. He turned to the left and then the right. *These pants make me look like a logger.* He took them off, tossing them onto the bed with every other pair of pants he owned.

His mom appeared in the doorway. "You look nice."

Patrick looked down at his white dress shirt (not flannel), green tie, and gray vest. He had on his boxers and reindeer socks. "I have no pants."

Mom stared at the pile on the bed.

"All of them look terrible."

"Pick your most comfortable," she said, taking a seat in the guest chair.

"That'd be jeans. I can't wear jeans on our first date."

She wrapped the blanket from the back of the chair around her shoulders. "Why not? I wore hot pink culottes on my first date with your father."

He groaned. "Thankfully, I don't own any culottes." Patrick opened his dresser drawer. He slipped on his favorite jeans, tucked in his shirt, and took a look in the mirror. He looked good. "Are you sure you'll be okay alone tonight?"

She nodded. "Honestly, I could use the rest. Are you nervous?"

He sucked in a deep breath. "That obvious?"

His mom moved in front of Patrick with a look of knowledge, love, and acceptance in her eye. She adjusted his tie. "Only to me. Do you know where you're going tonight?"

"No idea. He's surprising me." He glanced at his watch. "And he'll be picking me up in a few minutes."

His mom rested her hands on his shoulders and gave

him a supportive squeeze. "You deserve the very best. You're smart, kind, strong, and you'll make a great dad someday."

Patrick closed his eyes, dropping his head backward. "Don't start in on that."

"No pressure."

"I'm sure you'll get grandkids soon enough with Dolan and his new fiancée." Patrick couldn't stop the biting comment from flying out of his mouth.

"Maybe, but I always thought you'd—I shouldn't say it, but I always thought you'd make an incredible father."

Patrick hugged her, grateful for the vote of confidence.

After he released her, she gave him a small smile. "If you could do me a favor and try with Dolan."

Why? Why am I always the one who has to bend? "Honestly, I don't know if I'm capable of doing that with him."

She squeezed his arm. "You can do anything that you put your mind to." With that parting shot, his mom left.

After all these years, his mom still knew how to guilt him into doing anything. The doorbell rang, and he hurried to the front door. He swung it open expecting to see Sandy, but instead Chelsea stood in front of him. A light dusting of snow covered their stocking cap and jacket. They came in and shut the door behind them.

"Is everything okay?"

They rolled their lips into their mouth making them look like a flustered Kermit the Frog.

Something was off. Patrick placed his hands on his hips, going into action mode. "What happened?"

They inhaled and averted their eyes to the ceiling. "He can't come pick you up, so I'm here."

Really? That's it. This doesn't make sense. "I think I'm missing pieces to the puzzle here . . . "

"Put your stuff on and let's go."

While Patrick put on his boots, Moonshine nudged against his shoestrings. "You stay here and watch over Mom." He tussled the hair on the dog's head and then shrugged into his jacket.

Carefully meandering the streets, Chelsea drove their truck over the fresh powder. Patrick loved everything about his neighborhood this time of year, from the giant floppy snowman that never quite had enough air in it to the house with the three reindeer on the roof where Rudolph was replaced with a teddy bear with makeshift horns and a red-light bulb for its nose. And his favorite of them all: the blinking house with synchronized music. Sure, all of it was ridiculous, but Patrick enjoyed these quirks of his small town. Personally, he favored the colorful Christmas lights outlining his own house with an old-fashioned Santa's workshop on his front yard. Simple, classic, and cute.

Chelsea parked in front of the store. Patrick couldn't contain his questions any longer. "What are we doing here? Are we meeting here and then going to dinner?"

They gave him a blank look. "Go in."

The store was completely dark, which was unusual considering that a few lights always stayed on, and during the holidays a few of the Christmas lights remained on after closing. As Patrick moved, a set of luminary bags lit up on the stairs. A rush of excitement ran through him. He liked the unexpected, and this was certainly falling into that category. Even though he really wanted to race up the stairs, he took his time walking. His stomach flipped. He couldn't remember the last time someone had taken the time to romance him. When he reached the top step, he spotted a table set for two. The Christmas paper plates and tablecloth were whimsical and a bit absurt, just like Sandy.

Patrick glanced around, seeking out his dinner companion. A weird noise, sounding like a hiccup, broke the silence. A few seconds went by, and then the hiccup happened again. He turned around, wondering where the squeak was coming from. The next hiccup came out in a series, and then it dawned on Patrick that the small sound came from under the table. Who or what had taken shelter there? Patrick flipped up the tablecloth and bent down to look.

In the dim lighting, he had to squint to see, but was that Sandy? He blinked several times. It was! Why was his quirky date for the night huddled in the cramped space like a lost child with his knees drawn up to his chest? What the hell was going on? He dropped to his haunches to assess the situation and tried for a gentle smile. "Hello, there. What's happened?"

Sandy made a humming sound as if that tiny radio impression helped him navigate through his haze. His eyes opened absurdly wide. "What?"

Confused, he wiped a hand across his face. "Take my hand."

Sandy slapped his hand into Patrick's. He got a solid grip

and guided him out from under the table then helped him to his feet.

The weight of the other man flopped into Patrick's arms like a sack of potatoes. "You're a very stroup-stra-strapping man." Sandy leaned his head on Patrick's chest.

Chelsea and Sam came up the stairs carrying the Spanish tapas board and soup.

"Let's get some food in him." Sam placed the board in the middle of the table.

"What happened to him?" Patrick backed Sandy's wobbly body into a chair. Hopefully, he wouldn't fall face first into his food.

Chelsea shrugged as they placed the bowls down, and then Sam ladled out the soup.

"Everything was going well, and then the next thing we knew he'd consumed a pan of my special brownies. Then we found him doing shots and dancing at the bar."

He's not just drunk, but drunk and stoned off his ass. Patrick let out a growl of annoyance.

"This jingles my bells so hard. I want to take this bread to bed." Sandy stuffed the entire slice of baguette into his mouth, followed by picking up the entire triangle of brie, and taking a huge bite out of it. As if that wasn't enough, he held his bowl of soup and tried to drink it like a cappuccino.

Carefully, Sam grabbed the bowl and placed it on the table. "Stop, you don't want to burn yourself."

Sporting a goofy grin, Sandy made a finger gun and shot it at her.

After his incredibly difficult day, an inebriated date was

the last thing Patrick wanted to deal with. But Sam was right. Sandy needed to sober up, and food would help move that process along. Patrick removed his jacket and took a seat. "This really looks amazing. Thank you both. It means a lot to me."

"Not a problem. I have a main course prepared, so we'll let you get started on this, and then we'll check in with you." Sam turned to head back downstairs.

Chelsea patted his shoulder in commiseration before trailing after Sam.

Across the table from Patrick, Sandy tried to spoon soup in his mouth, but the liquid kept spilling off.

If they were going to get anywhere tonight, Patrick needed to help him. He smeared a piece of bread with olive tapenade and then added meat and cheese. He tapped Sandy's arm. When his befuddled date looked up, his features turned dreamy at the loaded tapas. Patrick prepared another plate of treats and set it in front of Sandy.

After a moment of successfully getting food into his mouth, Sandy seemed to take note of Patrick sitting across from him. "How did you do today? How today—how was your day today?"

At this point, Patrick could spout any nonsense, and he doubted that Sandy would remember a word of it tomorrow. "I went golfing with Blitzen, then the elves let me join their bowling league, and then I screwed Santa—overall pretty awesome."

"Sounds unbub . . . unbublievable." Sandy chewed and then guzzled his water.

Patrick took a spoonful of the wonderful soup. He looked up at Sandy, who had stopped chewing. Sandy's lips turned down and his face turned green. *He doesn't look well.* Patrick stepped quickly to Sandy and got him to his feet. Sandy slapped his hand over his mouth. Together they ran to the men's bathroom. Sandy sprinted to the first stall. Patrick stopped at the door. The sound of Sandy getting sick turned his stomach.

"Can I get you anything?"

The groan Sandy made was a cross between embarrassment and pain.

"I'm going to give you a minute." Patrick stepped out of the bathroom.

Sam and Chelsea stood by the table looking uncomfortable.

Unsure of what to say, he rubbed the back of his neck. "Hey, um, he's not doing so well. Would you mind taking care of all of this? I should probably get him home."

With a nod, Chelsea started the clean-up.

"I'm so sorry. Let us know if you need help getting him downstairs." Sam tossed the plates into the trash.

He thanked them and put on his jacket. After picking up Sandy's stuff, he retrieved Sandy from the bathroom and took the elevator down. Hopefully, Sandy had gotten everything out of his system. Patrick didn't want to make a big deal out of Sandy getting stoned, but he was hurt, and he didn't understand why he'd pull such a stupid stunt on their big night.

After stuffing Sandy into the backseat, he considered the

disastrous evening as he drove home. *Is this a routine for Sandy? Why do I get involved with men like this?*

He pulled up to his house and went through the drag-and-carry-the-stoned-man saga all over again. Once they were inside, Patrick helped Sandy out of his coat and boots before Sandy stumbled into the living room. As he turned to go to the couch, he tripped and knocked the small Dickensian village off its display table, causing it to crash to the ground. And then he fell face first onto the couch.

Stunned, Patrick stared in horror at the demolished village, feeling like it was his heart that had been dumped on the carpet. *I deserve better than this. It's Spencer all over again.*

CHAPTER 13

A pounding headache woke Sandy. His face stuck to the leather of the couch and a puddle of drool had formed under his mouth. As he opened his eyes, he tried to remember what had happened the night before. When he came up blank, he pushed himself up off the couch. In his balled-up hand was a tiny town crier. Sandy glanced at the carpet and the tiny Victorian village. He blinked himself awake. It was still dark outside, because it was the Midwest, but early enough that Patrick would be getting up soon.

Fudge. I got sloshed to the gills. I got stoned, took out a wee village and . . . Sandy poked his tongue around his mouth and lips. *Threw up. He saw me toss my cookies. Fantastic.* Sandy dropped his head into his hands. The room spun. How could he explain to Patrick what happened? And would he even want to hear it? He shook his head in slow motion.

The front door swung open, and Patrick stepped in

wearing his running gear, sweating, and panting. He closed the door, barely glancing in Sandy's direction. *Who could blame him?* Patrick stuffed his outerwear in the closet and headed for his bedroom. *Well, that's just terrific.*

Sandy began to clean up the mess on the floor. How the ceramic manor, pub, and inn had stayed intact was a freakin' Christmas miracle that only Santa could deliver. He laid the thick roll of fake snow on the table and proceeded to put the village back together again.

A loud blender roared to life in the kitchen and Sandy jumped, almost dropping the miniature light post he held in his hands. He winced and pressed a hand to his chest. And he wanted to hold one to his head considering how unbelievably loud that machine was.

Patrick turned off the blender, dumped in a banana, peanut butter, milk, and some kind of horrible looking powder, and then started the mixer again.

He returned to his task of recreating the Christmas village.

Patrick increased the torture by adding blocks of ice to the blender. Sandy guessed it was to get even with him for last night, but he couldn't be certain.

When Patrick stopped punishing him with the annoying kitchen appliance, Sandy met his gaze. "Only takes one gay man to take out a village," he said, attempting to lighten the tension between them.

Patrick removed the blender's cover and tossed it in the sink. With a seething look, he poured the nasty-looking concoction into a large plastic cup.

Evidently, humor's off the table. Sandy continued to pick up each piece of the village set and place it back in the order he remembered from his first day in the house. He loved the inconsistency of this athletic, serious guy having a quirky thing for ceramics and Victorian villages. It was cute . . . and so endearing. *I really need to try to fix this.*

Rather than look Patrick directly in the eye, Sandy turned the town crier over in his hands. "I'm sorry for last night." In a misguided attempt to make his issues disappear, he'd embarrassed himself. And hurt Patrick. It was foolish and juvenile to do something stupid like getting stoned and drunk. That's not how life worked. He couldn't drug or drink away his problems because they were always there the next day, lurking. Or, in Sandy's case, angrily gulping a chalky protein shake.

"Why?"

Sandy didn't understand his response. "Why am I sorry? Or why did I do it?"

"Yeah." The muscles in Patrick's jaw clenched with barely contained anger. "Let's start with why you're sorry."

He inhaled a deep breath and set the Christmas figure on the fake snow. "Because I ruined our night, made a complete ass out of myself, and put you in a shitty position."

"Do you know what I'm going through right now?"

"I know your Dad's in the hospital and the store's finances are in the tank." Sandy rubbed his head. He wasn't supposed to know everything about Dolan, but he did, so he could at least fess up to that bit. "I've been filled in on some of what went down with your brother. And I know my timing last night was shitty. I should've been supportive and instead, I made everything worse."

"Yesterday was a disaster, having to see Dolan after ten years. I showed up last night, looking forward to spending time with you. I changed my pants about eight hundred times. I wore a fucking tie."

Sandy liked the casual, yet very Patrick ensemble he wore last night. "I remember. The green of the tie made your eyes pop."

Patrick sighed. He set his shake down and folded his arms like he didn't know how to respond.

"And now for the 'why'". Sandy inched a few paces toward Patrick, unsure how close he should get. "I screwed up. I got scared."

Surprise flickered through that amazing green of Patrick's eyes.

"I'm not scared of you, but I was scared of having a date when I haven't had a real date in years, or at least one that I wanted to be a real date. And it freaked me out in a way that was new for me. I didn't want to let you down because you have so many things in your life that . . . " Sandy didn't know how to finish that sentence, especially since he would seriously let Patrick down if he ever found out about his photography job. "And then I did let you down. I don't deserve to know someone like you let alone go out with someone like you."

Patrick ran a hand across his forehead. "Don't do that. Don't idealize me. I make a ton of mistakes. It doesn't matter that you haven't had a real relationship in a long time, or if ever. I like you as you are, messy with a tendency toward disaster. But you're cute and funny and always put me in a better mood."

Sandy's heart raced. He took a couple of steps forward. "I do?"

"Yeah . . . but tell me when you're freaked out. We can talk about stuff. And maybe we don't date."

Sandy squished his brows together. That wasn't quite what he was aiming for.

"Let's call it something else," Patrick elaborated.

"Something fabulous, but not too fabulous that it freaks me out?"

"Why not?"

"Oh, how about a meeting?"

"What?"

"Yes! It's a meeting. A covert, sexy, Santa and elf meeting." Sandy stepped up to Patrick and played with the bottom of his shirt. "Wow. You smell."

The corners of Patrick's mouth rose in a grin. "That's what happens when you run five miles."

This guy and his exercising. Ugh.

"You should join me sometime."

Sandy would rather be forced to wear more flannel. "I'm not what one would call athletic."

"Hiking?"

"That's the walking through the woods thing? Pass. I don't like creepy crawly things that could potentially bite me on the ankles and cause my death."

"But in the winter, there's no chance of that at all."

"You say that, but I bet in some rare instance there'd be a hibernating spider that decided to wake up and zero in on my boot, crawl into my sock, and gnaw into my skin to the bone and kill me." He folded his arms and tapped his foot.

Patrick shook his head. "Only you would come up with something that outrageous."

"What's your plan for the day?" Sandy leaned a hand on the countertop as Patrick cleaned up the clutter from his shake.

"I'm going to drive Mom to the hospital and pop in to see Dad. Then I want to be in the store today. It's been awesome having Chels and you cover, but I need to run some figures and check on sales."

"Perfect. After the toy drive, I can steal you away for some McCormick TikToks, too."

Patrick groaned.

"Don't worry. It'll be short blurbs and if Chelsea can do it . . ." Sandy threw a hand in the air as if that was the end of that discussion.

"It's not that. It's the toy drive. I forgot about it."

"No worries. We got Sam to volunteer."

"Awesome, but I'm Santa. I have to be there during the delivery to some of the homes. We have a list of families who asked for Santa specifically. Mom will have to drive to the hospital on her own this morning."

Sandy rolled his fingers across the countertop. "You might hate this, but what if you close the store for just a couple of hours for the Santa delivery portion?"

Patrick took a moment as he leaned his palms behind him. "I think it's our only solution."

Colleen walked out of the guest room fully dressed and ready to go. "Good morning to you both. What are we thinking about for breakfast?" She crossed over to the coffee pot and then filled up the glass container with water.

"I grabbed a protein shake. I'm good."

"You're not good." His mother raised an eyebrow at him. "I'm going to make something, and we'll all sit down at the table. Understood?"

Patrick shook his head. A glimmer of a smile graced his lips.

"I vote for anything super greasy. But first a shower." Sandy could smell the alcohol rising out of his pores. He pecked Patrick on the lips before darting off to Patrick's room. Okay, he royally screwed up his date with Patrick on purpose. But today was a new day, and it sounded like Patrick forgave him or maybe just decided to forget. Either way, he couldn't stop himself from whistling "Baby It's Cold Outside" as he gathered his things for the bathroom. *Hopefully, it won't be cold for much longer.*

———

Patrick handed his mother a carton of eggs from the refrigerator.

"Is this your way of avoiding Dolan?" she asked as she started cracking the eggs into a bowl.

He ran a hand over his beard. *No, it was a perk of my busy day.* "It's better if Dad doesn't have too many people visiting at once, and I have a lot on my schedule today." He didn't know how to talk to his mom about Dolan. His brother had broken his trust, and it would take a lot more than an expensive jacket and suit to change his mind. "Will you promise me that you'll be careful with Dolan?"

She turned to him, giving him a pained look. "What exactly do you think he's plotting?"

That was it. He didn't know what his brother was up to, but he wanted to be ready when the other shoe dropped. "For instance, what about the business?"

"What about it?" She poured the eggs into a pan.

"Does he plan to be involved? Is he willing to invest and help save the store that he sank? Or at least pay the money back?" He folded his arms, stewing in the anger that returned whenever he thought of Dolan.

"Would you consider working with him if he decided to return to the business? You can't run both stores by yourself. You'll need help." She gave him a side-eye as she moved the eggs.

Is that something they've already talked about? Fuck. Fuck. Fuck. "Is Dad planning to retire?"

She inhaled. "Honey, he needs to slow down. We both do. This episode wasn't the best way to get us to realize this, but we're not going to live forever. I had plans for us to go to Ireland next year, and now is the time for us to get a new manager at the Madison store. Dolan has experience."

Yeah, experience running off with the bankroll. "But what about his big job in the city?"

Her features twisted up. "We're family. We don't leave one another behind."

Of course not, we steal one another blind and then bolt for five years. The frustration rose in his body, and his shoulders tightened. "Have you and Dad talked about this already?"

"He's not strong enough. Mark my words: he will retire, or I will leave him. This is the end of the line."

This wasn't new. His mom had been threatening to divorce or leave his dad ever since Patrick was a kid. It was an empty threat, and everyone knew it. "Before you do that, can you wait for me to be there?"

She patted his cheek in a placating manner.

As soon as Sandy was done with his shower, Patrick slipped in and scrubbed down as quickly as possible. They ate, and then Patrick and Sandy jumped into the SUV with Moonshine to head to the store.

It was probably a mistake not going to the hospital when Dolan was there with their parents. His brother could manipulate them into anything without him if Patrick weren't there to keep an eye on his shenanigans. By the end of the day, he could be out of a job if Dolan talked his dad into closing the stores. The way his mom spoke, it sounded like she'd already considered something like that. If it ended up him having to work with Dolan, he'd lose his mind or be tossed in jail for strangling him. He was positive his dad didn't want to retire. He always told Patrick retirement was for quitters.

Sandy reached over and squeezed his knee. "Hey . . . you're doing some awfully heavy lifting over there with your thoughts. Care to share?"

"Dad, Mom, Dolan, the business. I'm worried about everything, and I can't stop going round and round with it all." His grip tightened on the steering wheel as if he was on the verge of breaking it in two.

"Maybe you should bring Dolan here and have it out with him? Put it all out there." Sandy rubbed a circle on Patrick's knee. The soothing gesture prompted him to ease up on the wheel.

It wasn't a horrible suggestion, if he could hold his temper and not squash Dolan's face like a snowball. "He's got a big cushy job in Chicago, so why would he want anything to do with the stores? Although, if the job is a complete fabrication, then he'll probably want to take us for a ride and get us to sell or go out of business to get some of the money."

"That's devious."

"That's Dolan." Patrick sighed as he parked the SUV behind the store.

"Let me play Scrooge's advocate here. What if that did happen?"

Patrick hit the steering wheel. "My parents would be crushed."

Sandy turned toward Patrick, nodding as if it wasn't all that bad. "But he'd probably never come back after that, and you, your parents would have less stress in your lives without the stores."

Patrick's mouth dropped open. He couldn't believe his ears.

Sandy held his hands in the air. "It's terrible, I know. The absolute worst of the worst. But look at where your dad is right now. He's recovering. And you're grinding your teeth and squeezing the steering wheel so hard that I'm afraid you're going to pop something, and it ain't gonna be pretty. It's really hard to see it now, because you're holding on to everything so tightly, but things happen the way they're supposed to happen for a reason."

Hearing the words, Patrick slowly relaxed against the headrest.

"It's the holiday season, and during this time of the year we're supposed to believe in hope and peace, right?"

Patick rolled his head to the right to look at Sandy. His comments made perfectly good sense, but he wasn't ready to give up yet. And he certainly wasn't ready to give up and hand everything over to Dolan. As lovely as Sandy's sentiment was, it didn't give him as much comfort as he needed. *What I need is defense. What I need is a plan.*

CHAPTER 14

After they arrived at the store, Patrick went upstairs to his admin work, and Sandy set up a spot near Chelsea's register to check on the store website and social media.

"Hey, look at this. We've had a bump in our analytics." He did a little dance, but Chelsea gave him their deadpan stare. "Okay, I know you're not all candy canes and holly jolly, but at least give me one whoo-hoo."

"Woo. Hoo."

A customer started to unload their basket, and Chelsea began the checkout process.

Sandy didn't want to take all the credit for the increase, but they'd already had a few more customers this morning, so that was a win for social media. At least, he hoped that was the case. He snapped his fingers as an idea formed.

He took his cell out of his back pocket. "Be right back," he mumbled to Chelsea as he headed to Patrick's office. He gave a rap on the door and swung it open.

Patrick glanced up from his computer.

"Ignore me." Sandy held his phone in the air. "Pretend I'm a ghost from Christmas present. I need some B-roll." Patrick didn't say anything, which was fine, but the level of concern on his twisted features showed the store was still struggling. Not that a day of social media and an upgrade to the website would instantly make the store money, but Sandy had high expectations.

As he filmed, he considered his mom's relationship with his stepdad and how smothering it was to be around. Oddly enough, in the past few days an outsider might say the same about how much time he was spending with Patrick and vice versa. *Maybe love wasn't so suffocating after all?* But inside, Sandy still hesitated and was fearful of a relationship beyond a few days, weeks, or months.

He stopped filming and walked out to the rail to view the customers below. He'd never been at the store during a real hustle and bustle. He imagined it would be amazing to see a holiday shopping scene like one out of a classic film. His heart ached the McCormick's loss of their store.

Patrick stepped up next to him.

"What about historic building grants or loans?" Sandy asked, knowing those were options that Patrick had probably already considered.

"We tried those, but we didn't qualify during the last round. We can apply again at the end of this year, but we can't rely on that for assistance." Patrick turned. "Ready to load the toys? Then we'll get into costume and take off."

Sandy nodded. "I'll have to skip the elf shoes. I don't think accelerating and braking in giant floppy felt shoes would work out. Unless you're okay with me plowing us into a tree while the bells jingle us all the all way."

Patrick's shoulders shook while leading them to the locker room.

Does he think I'm kidding about crashing? He's so adorbs it's disgusting. A tingle of anticipation ran up Sandy's spine.

———————

As Sandy consulted the printout of addresses Chelsea had supplied him with, Patrick turned the radio to a station with round the clock Christmas music. Punching in an address on his GPS, Sandy attempted to slide the phone into the holder. After his third try, Patrick yanked the device out of his hands and attached it to the housing.

A gooey sensation built up in Sandy's chest. "I have a confession," he said, turning to glance over at Patrick.

"Yeah? Is it a juicy one?" Patrick didn't have on his Santa beard and glasses, so when he leaned over the console his piercing green eyes held Sandy's with laser-like precision.

Sandy leaned in, too, resting his chin in his hand. He enjoyed being close to Patrick and smelling the pine-scented hunk. Today there was also a mix of peppermint candy. They'd given out so much sugar to the kids they visited that

Sandy was certain parents would call them in a month regarding dental bills. "I like being with you."

"I'm not a priest, but I've been in enough confessional booths to know that's not a juicy confession."

"I don't practice any religion, so I wouldn't know. But, how about this? I like that you volunteer and give so much to those around you."

Patrick's brows rose and wrinkles formed on his forehead. *Who knew wisdom lines could be sexy?*

"I've never been with a guy who thinks of others and takes action to change things."

"Having you here this year has made everything brighter. Dealing with Dad's health could've taken me to a dark place, but it didn't because of you." Patrick leaned forward and pressed a quick kiss to Sandy's mouth. "Thank you."

Sandy knew his cheeks had heated up, not just from the kiss, but also from the tenderness in Patrick's words. Sandy cleared the emotion building in his throat. "Santa, we better get this sleigh going, or we're never going to get everything done."

Patrick put on his beard and glasses. "That's right, my favorite elf."

Sandy started the SUV. As they traveled, they sang along to the holiday music inserting their own ridiculous lyrics and inuendoes. At each home, they met families in need. But what struck Sandy was the joy and gratitude he witnessed in each home. This was truly a Grinch heart-growing-three-sizes kind of event.

It was after dark when they rolled up to their last home,

an old, rundown farmhouse in the middle of nowhere. The frozen dirt-, ice-, and snow-packed road up to the home made for treacherous traveling. Sandy took his time as he followed Patrick to the front door to deliver the last of their gifts. They nearly fell on their butts while trying to get back to the vehicle. It was only when Sandy backed up the SUV too far to turn around in the driveway that they ran into a problem. The tires spun as he tried to maneuver them forward and out. He tried several times to no avail.

"It's official. We're stuck. Santa, you need more reindeer." Sandy leaned forward, against the steering wheel.

Patrick fished his phone from his pocket and FaceTimed Chelsea.

They immediately popped up on the screen. "Hey, what's up?"

"The magic of the Midwest got us. We're stuck." Sandy leaned over to get his face on screen.

"Roger that. I'm leaving my last house now. I'll swing over. Text me the address. Sam is done, and I told her we'd all meet up at the store afterward."

"See ya soon." Patrick ended the call.

"Sooo, what do we do to keep warm?" Sandy bounced his eyebrows, wishing for a make-out session in the backseat.

Patrick smirked. "As much as I like what you're thinking, which I'd bet is dirty, it's almost zero out. To be on the safe side we should go back inside."

Sandy let out a whine of protest. He put his elf hat back on. "They better have hot cocoa." And then he realized what he said. "Yes, I am that shallow. Although, I would take hot water. I may sound picky, but I'm not."

"Sure, sure, keep telling yourself that." Patrick attached his beard and glasses and adjusted his hat before opening the passenger door.

———

It was close to an hour by the time Chelsea showed up at the house. The family was kind enough to sit with them, and the kids absolutely loved having Santa and one of his elves for almost an entire evening. Patrick thought it was the best night ever, chatting with the kids and helping them put their toys together. If only he could have this kind of hands-on job where he helped people all the time. He could feel it made a difference for the family.

When they got outside after Chelsea arrived, Patrick removed his Santa get-up and attached the chain from Chelsea's truck onto the SUV. Once he gave Chelsea the thumbs up, he hopped into the truck and put it in neutral. Chelsea hit the gas, and the SUV popped out of the frozen snow like it was nothing. Patrick hopped out of the truck to remove the chain and place it in the truck bed.

"I'll follow you to the store," Chelsea said with a smirk.

"You think we're going to get stuck again?"

Chelsea gave a half-shrug and walked away.

Patrick smiled as he entered the SUV.

"What's so funny?"

"They think we're going to slide into the ditch on our way out."

Patrick hit the gas too hard, and the tires spun. He glanced at the dash. "In case you need to know, this button here is for the four-wheel drive."

Sandy covered his mouth. "Whoopsie?"

Patrick shook his head as he drove them away. His phone lit up on the dash from an unknown caller. Normally, he wouldn't accept a call from a number he didn't know, but since his dad was in the hospital, he hit the accept button.

"Patrick? Are you on the way back to the store?" Sam asked.

"Should be there in about a half hour."

"I don't want to alarm you, but my dad got a call to a store on Main Street. It's slippery out so don't rush or anything." Sam raised her voice as if she worried he might drive a hundred miles per hour on the unpredictable roads.

Is it a break in? Please tell me no one is hurt. Patrick's knuckles turned white as he squeezed the steering wheel. "Thanks for the heads up. See ya soon." He ended the call.

"Are you okay to drive?" Sandy asked.

"Fine. It's probably nothing. During the winter we get power surges. We have to be careful about the pipes freezing."

Sandy flagged a hand in the air. "That doesn't sound so bad."

Patrick gave him a side-eye. "Say that when you're standing in water over your ankles."

"Oh, fucking hell."

He took his time driving, enjoying the music in the background and his driving companion. It was the simple things he liked about getting to know Sandy. His flair for the dramatic. His sense of humor. *Maybe I could do a sneaky date and make him dinner at the house?* "Do you like corned beef?"

Sandy turned in Patrick's direction. "That's the sexiest question I've ever been asked. Saucy!"

"I'm serious. After the amazing dinner you had Sam create the other night, I know you're probably a foodie, so?" Patrick's culinary skills were on the low end, but he grilled a mean smoked corned beef brisket that was damn tasty.

"I'd die for corned beef." Sandy clapped his hands and wiggled with excitement.

"You're killing me."

As Patrick turned onto Main Street, a barricade was up and there were a couple of police cars. He pulled over and parked. His phone buzzed.

"What's going on?" Sandy forward, trying to see around the cars and people gathered on the street.

His mom's face appeared on the screen. He accepted the call as he and Sandy climbed out of the SUV. The smell of smoke nearly overwhelmed him. His eyes stung from the scent and ash in the air. "Hey, Mom, can't talk now . . . I probably won't make visiting hours. Give Dad a hug from me."

Chelsea ran up to him. "Something caught fire."

"I gotta go, Mom." He hung up and jogged toward the gathering.

All three of them moved through the crowd to get a better look. Sam was by the barricade with her dad, the sheriff.

"Sam?" Patrick called out, but not loud enough for her to hear over all the commotion.

Chelsea flapped their arms over their head to get Sam's attention.

She pulled on her dad's sleeve and pointed to the group.

Patrick's stomach sank as the implications of the situation hit him. This couldn't be good.

Sheriff Gómez waved them over. "Let these three through," he said to the officer fending off the crowd.

The sheriff led Patrick and Sandy down the street, with Chelsea and Sam behind them. Silently, the group passed fire engines and firefighters. As they moved down the block, smoke became thicker making it more difficult to breathe. The sick feeling in Patrick's stomach intensified. Once the McCormick's building came into view, his eyes stung with tears. The building was still standing, but the damage was done. McCormick's General Store was destroyed.

Oh my God. Patrick's shoulders dropped. It was as if someone had reached into his breath chest and stolen his breath away. The shock of it all was too much to handle.

"What the actual fuck?" Sandy placed a hand on Patrick's shoulder. "Are you—obviously not okay—I don't even know what to say."

Chelsea stepped up to Sheriff Gómez. "Any word on what happened? How it started?"

The sheriff flagged Chief Lang stepped over to the group.

"Awfully sorry, Patrick. We got here as fast as possible. Unfortunately, it was already too far gone."

"What . . . how could this . . . ?" Patrick couldn't fathom what was in shambles before him.

Sandy took his hand and squeezed it. "Can you tell us anything?" he asked the chief.

"Arson. An accelerant was dumped haphazardly about. The first and second floors took the most damage. The third has smoke and water damage. We'll have an investigator take a deeper dive, but we found some burned-out gas cans inside the store." The chief glanced at all the faces in their group. "As far as I understand, the store was closed this afternoon?"

Patrick nodded, still staring at the building in shock.

"We closed down for the toy drive," Chelsea replied.

"Why would someone do this?" Patrick finally met the eyes of the chief.

"I'll be working closely with the fire investigator. And I can't believe I'm going to ask this clichéd question, but was anyone angry or upset with you, your family, or the store?" Sheriff Gómez hitched his hands onto his utility belt like an old west gunslinger.

Patrick debated the question. Dolan came to mind, but would he do something this horrible? Did he have the capacity to destroy a family store? And why? But Dolan was nearby, and he imagined that his mom had shared with Dolan the financial issues. He couldn't tell the Sheriff about Dolan. Not yet. He'd talk to his brother first. Patrick shook his head.

"What about that guy you fired?" Sandy asked.

Patrick turned to Sandy. "Who?" The past few days were a blur.

"He's talking about Wayne," Chelsea supplied.

The sheriff and chief exchanged looks.

"He came to work loaded, so I fired him." Patrick furrowed his brow. He couldn't believe Wayne could ever be sober enough to try something like this, and it didn't seem like he held a grudge, but who knew at this point?

"Chelsea called me about an incident at the store with him." The sheriff flipped open his notebook. "Drunk and sleeping it off in the locker room."

Patrick released Sandy's hand. This was all news to him. He turned his attention to Sandy and Chelsea. "Why didn't either one of you tell me about this?"

"I texted you." Chelsea added as if that explained everything.

"You were with your dad, and you probably missed it." Sandy shrugged.

"I turned him away from Ace's that morning. I gave him some coffee and sat him at a table, but when I returned, he'd taken off," Sam explained.

The sheriff wrote more notes in his book. "I'll swing by his house and talk to him. But if any of you think of anything else, please let me know." He tucked his black pad into his pocket.

Patrick gave a quick nod. How was he going to tell his dad and mom about this? They'd be shocked. He'd talk to his mom tonight. He'd have to call the insurance company and the bank and the vendors and about a million other places. Maybe they could wait a few days to tell his dad? The stomach churning returned. This was officially his worst nightmare come true.

Sandy removed his scarf and wrapped it around Patrick's neck. "I don't know if you're in shock, but you're even more white than usual, so I'm going to say, yes, you are in shock, and so I'm putting this on you to help warm you up. Damn. It's cold out here." Sandy looked to Sam and Chelsea.

"Let's go next door," Chelsea said, pointing at Ace's.

The next thing he knew, Sandy was looping his arm through his, and Sam took the other side. *He might be right. Maybe I am in shock because my feet feel like they're stuck in blocks of ice.*

CHAPTER 15

Ace's was relatively busy with patrons walking in after the excitement of the fire. Sandy stood at the bar with Chelsea, waiting for their drinks. He cast a concerned gaze in Patrick's direction. Sam had placed a blanket around his shoulders.

"This has to be killing him." The words left Sandy's mouth before he could stop himself. "If I hadn't gotten us stuck, we might have been able to stop the person."

"Or gotten yourselves hurt." Chelsea provided a darker perspective.

He hadn't thought of that. He'd be crushed if anything happened to Patrick.

"It's not your fault. Whoever did this held a grudge or was angry at the McCormicks for something. It's a good thing you got stuck." Chelsea picked up their root beer and Sam's cranberry juice and carried the drinks to their table.

Sandy followed with his hot toddy and an Irish coffee for Patrick. He had no idea if Patrick liked spiked caffeinated drinks, but since he still had that ice-glazed-over look on his face, Sandy figured this might help the thawing process. He rested the drinks on the table and sat as close as possible to Patrick, figuring he could use the body heat.

Scooting Patrick's mug closer to him, he encouraged him to sip the warm beverage. Sandy didn't know what to think or what to do with Patrick, who had shut down completely. He wasn't talking. He was barely blinking. It was odd to see the normally active man power down to a halt.

"Wonder how someone got in . . . " Chelsea mumbled aloud.

"The front door was locked. I saw you lock it." Sam took a drink of her juice.

"Do you want to call your parents?" He leaned close to Patrick so only he could hear him.

Patrick blinked and turned to Sandy. "Dad can't know yet. Mom should be on her way to my house." His robotic response was followed by chugging down half the hot coffee.

He grabbed the cup from Patrick. "Maybe not all in one gulp." He set the mug back on the table.

Patrick inhaled and leaned back, tightening the blanket around his shoulders. "I can't believe this happened before Christmas. There're so many calls to make." It appeared that the Irish coffee had brought Patrick back to the living.

"Don't worry about any of that. We can help you sort through whatever you need tomorrow." Sandy had no idea what that entailed, but he was certain that anyone at this table or even in the bar would jump at a chance to help Patrick and his family. Everything that Patrick's family and the store did for the community was always a good thing.

"We owe so much at the bank. The insurance will cover the loss, but I have no idea how we're going to pay off all the debt."

"Don't you have that fund set up?" Sam leaned her elbows on the table.

"I told her about it," Chelsea hooked a thumb in Sam's direction.

"We do. That should help. I can update the page tonight and the social media." Patrick might squash the idea, but Sandy would include details about the fire. Now, more than ever, he wanted to be there for Patrick.

"Not to make things worse . . . my dad will find out about the financial stuff with Dolan and the possible eviction. Be up front about it," Sam said.

"It's not a secret," Chelsea added.

"Yup, the entire town knows that the store wasn't doing so hot. Especially after I had to lay off the majority of the staff in the fall. If your dad needs bank records or anything, I have them." Patrick folded his arms and straightened his shoulders, evolving from defeat into a defensive mode.

"Don't go crazy when he interviews you is all I'm saying," Sam continued.

That hit Patrick wrong, and his chest puffed up. "What are you saying? Does he think I started the fire?"

Chelsea lifted a hand in front of Patrick like a stop sign. "Not what she means."

"It's part of the process." Sam fidgeted and shifted in her seat. "They have to clear the closest most obvious suspect before looking at others."

Abruptly, Patrick stood, tipping his chair over. He tossed the blanket on the table, barely missing the drinks. "I'm done commiserating." He turned and stomped toward the door.

Sandy sighed, uncertain if he should stay or go.

"Go after him." Chelsea jerked their chin toward the angry Patrick.

"Thank you both. He's still, well, I'm not sure . . .. "

Sam gave him a small smile. "We get it. Go on."

Patrick was halfway to the SUV before Sandy caught sight of him. "Wait up," he shouted, hitting a slippery patch. Surprisingly, Patrick stopped.

Out of breath, he half walked and half jogged the rest of the way. "They were only trying to prepare you. They're your friends, you know? No need to skewer them with an icicle." With the still smoky air filling his lungs, Sandy's breath came out in a puff against the cold air.

Patrick rubbed a hand against his face. "It's freezing out here. Let's keep moving."

Once inside the car, Patrick flipped on the heat and the seat warmers. "Please don't ask me if I'm alright or to keep my emotions in check, because I'm not and I can't. I've lost my business, my job, and, from the conversation with Sam, I'm the number one suspect, so don't."

Sandy buckled his safety belt. "Fine. But I'm gonna say

you're acting like a drama queen, and this is coming from the queeny-ist of queens."

"Don't you get it? I lost everything tonight."

"That's the most fucked up thing you could ever say. Chelsea, Sam, me, your family, and all the people in this sleepy town are here for you. You didn't lose everything. What happened is horrible, but you have so much to give and so do the people around you." Sandy placed a hand on Patrick's knee. "Right now, the only thing you need to do is breathe. Take this one day at a time because this only happened tonight, and you can't go around like a robot one minute and get pissed with people who have your best interest at heart the next."

Ever so slowly, Patrick placed his hand on top of Sandy's. "I'm worried."

"That's absolutely shocking. Tell me something I don't know." His voice dripped with sarcasm.

"I neglected to tell the sheriff that Dolan is in town."

Sandy considered this, but this was such a nefarious act. "Would he really go this batshit cray-cray?"

Patrick looked over the dash as if considering the question. "Who knows? I never thought he'd screw over the family, rob us blind and run off with all the cash either." He put the car in drive and pulled away from the curb.

"Try not to let that old, giant, gaping wound be the motivation for you to smack your brother in the kisser. And to be smart, we'll do some internet investigating on your bro tonight. Tomorrow I'll go with you to the hospital. You'll visit with your dad. And then calmly—

emphasis on the Zen here—have a convo with your brother."

The dim light didn't hide Patrick's Angry Birds expression.

I'm going to have to break up a fight, aren't I? I'll just have to remember not to wear white to this shitshow. As the potent scent of smoke infected the car, Sandy's heart tugged. Any of the people Patrick cared about could've been in the store when this happened. His mom and stepdad and Julia popped into his head. He dug his phone out of his elf suit and dashed off some heartfelt texts. Sure, it was maybe overly emotional due to a terrible event that completely missed him, but 'tis the season for over-the-top responses. He could always blame his sentimentality on the hot toddy later, but for now, he was glad he'd sent the texts.

As Patrick pulled into his driveway, Sandy's phone rang. No one ever called except his mom. He pulled the device out of his pocket and peered at the goofy photo of her and Harley. "It's my mom."

He hit the accept button. "Why are you calling?"

"You write a message like you're dying. Are you dying? Harley is a good doctor. You'll go to him. He will fix you."

"He's a sports doc. If I had a sprained ankle, I might go to him." *If forced by jockstrap.* He swung open the car door.

"See, the boy is fine," Harley's voice bellowed in the background. Naturally, his mom had them on speaker.

Sandy palmed his cheek with a hand as he entered Patrick's house. Sometimes, like now, he doubted that his mom was his biological mother. "How is 'I love you' synonymous with death?"

"I thought it was code. You're not ill?"

Not unless we're counting how sick of this conversation I am. "Not at all."

"Good. Then why did you call?"

Sandy sat down on the bench and began to untie his boots. This was a typical response from her. She always forgot who called who and why.

"Since we got you on the phone, do you want ham or deep-fried turkey this year? My cousin sent me a new rub that I'd like to try out on y'all." His stepdad must have stepped closer to the phone because his baritone voice boomed like it was in surround sound.

"Delicious. Have at it." He slipped out of his jacket and hung it up. Since Patrick must've gone to his room, Sandy took a seat on the couch. He never talked to his mom about relationships, but maybe this was an opportunity to give it a shot. "I, ah, I met someone . . . "

His mom let out her high-pitched happy squeak.

"Alright, alright, alright." His stepdad was always surprisingly cool with him being gay, which threw him off momentarily.

He leaned forward, resting his elbows on his knees, amused at Harley's terrible impression of Wooderson from *Dazed and Confused.* "Okay, let's not go getting too excited. We've been spending a lot of time together, and I like it, but it's new, different."

"You're scared," his mom added. "Don't be scared."

He almost had to laugh at how simple his mom always made things out to be. "But what if I'm keeping something from him?"

"Shucks, tell him. Tell him how you feel and about whatever it is. You gotta stand up and speak your truth to him."

"What if he hates me for it?" Sandy dropped his voice down low.

His mom didn't entertain the notion for a second. "Impossible. You're likable."

"That's right," Harley confirmed.

His mom and Harley always tag-teamed him with their responses. That's what weirded him out. He didn't know if he'd ever be ready for this kind of sympatico banter. "You do know that you're both annoying."

"How are we annoying? We are a super team. You could be a super team if you would get over yourself."

Sandy scoffed at the accusation. "That's just it—you two gush all over one another all the time, and it's disgusting and alienating."

His parents turned silent. He didn't mean to say those hurtful words aloud to them, but they managed to slip out. He was a giant asshat who didn't deserve love. "I'm sorry. I didn't mean to say that at all."

Harley cleared his throat. "I love your mother. And I love you. We only ever wanted to show you how much."

"After you-know-who left . . . " His mom spoke of his bio dad as if he were a fictional villain from an alternate dimension. "I thought that the next time I find love that I would share it. Whoever loved me would love you as much as I do.

You were not supposed to feel left out but embraced by it. By us. By our love."

That hit Sandy right in the chest. *I'm a horrible human being.* "Mom, Dad . . . I'm, I'm so stupid . . . "

"You can be a might bit thick sometimes." Harley's belly laugh was loud enough to shake the windows.

"I agree. Your grades were always bad," his mom chimed in as if his elementary school grades had anything to do with the conversation.

He exhaled a deep breath and sat up. "Enough of you HIlarious people. I'm hanging up now." He hit the end call button. Sandy stood up, determined to make time tomorrow to have a serious conversation with Patrick about his photography job with the evil company. He didn't plan to kick Patrick while he was down, but maybe, like his parents, they could get through this together.

———

In the morning Patrick and Sandy swung by the store to confirm that the damage looked as bad in the daylight as it had the night before. It did.

Discouraged, they dropped Moonshine off with Chelsea, who was willing to take the dog for the day while they were at the hospital. His mom had taken the news surprisingly well last night. She was glad that no one was hurt. "It's only a building," she said as she hugged him and then Sandy. They agreed not to say anything to his dad until the doctor gave the okay.

As Patrick and Sandy escorted his mom into the hospital, he recalled Sandy's encouraging words from last night and concluded that he was right. He had friends and family. Losing the store was hard, but they'd get through this ordeal.

In the elevator up to his dad's room, Patrick slipped his hand into Sandy's. "Thank you for last night. I appreciate you."

Sandy turned to meet his eyes. "Whatever you need. I'm here. Maybe later we could sneak away and have a conversation? There's something I need to talk to you about." A worrisome crease formed on Sandy's forehead as his brows came together.

Patrick didn't want to worry about one more thing than he already had on his plate, but he nodded and the doors to their floor opened. He released Sandy's hand, but the peacefulness of being near Sandy lingered with him until he walked into his dad's hospital room and saw Dolan. *That didn't last more than a minute. Damn it.*

Everyone said their hellos with hugs, but Patrick wasn't about to hug his brother. And he couldn't wait a second longer to talk to him. He needed to know if he was involved in the arson, and he needed to know now. "Hey, let's step out for a minute."

Their mom shot him a pair of warning eyes. He held up a hand to imply that everything was fine.

"I'll go with them." Sandy patted his mom's hand as he followed behind them.

"Why's he coming? I don't even know that guy?" Dolan

asked, as Patrick led them to an empty waiting room down the hall from his dad's room.

"He's a friend," Patrick grunted.

"All right, what's up, Bro?" Dolan crossed his hands in front of himself like an altar boy during communion.

If he uses the word bro one more time, I will ram a reindeer horn up his ass. "Where were you yesterday?"

Dolan's features bunched up. "Where do you think? Here."

"You didn't leave at all? Not even to get food or call your girlfriend or text a shady character?" Patrick folded his arms, watching for any signs of deception on Dolan's face.

"I ran out for food in the afternoon because Ma and I are sick of the cafeteria slop. What the hell is going on?"

"There was a fire at the store."

Dolan's brows lifted upward in what looked like surprise, but Patrick had been fooled before. "How long were you gone?"

"You think I did this? You think that I could do something like this?" Dolan pointed a finger at himself with his voice raised.

"Yeah, I do," Patrick yelled back at his brother.

Sandy stepped closer to Patrick. "Okay, so everyone take a beat. Get Zen. Pray to Buddha or Santa or Frosty or whatevs for a hot sec, and remember we're in a hospital." Sandy made a slight turn toward Dolan. "Here's the facts, the sheriff will need to talk to you. And let's be honest, your shady past will be revealed, so if you have a receipt you should be fine, especially since there are a zillion cameras inside and outside of this place. And possibly from where you picked up the food."

"I do and they will."

Sandy brushed his palms together like he was dusting off imaginary lint. "Excellent. We'll need to see it."

As if I'm going to take his word for it. "And to make certain you didn't pay someone to do the dirty work—you're going to hand over all your devices to the cops." Patrick raised a brow at Dolan.

CHAPTER 16

Sandy crossed his fingers that these two tall, muscular men didn't come to blows any second, because there was absolutely no way he'd be able to prevent a bloodbath with his diminutive stature and jelly upper arms.

"Is everything ruined in the store? Is it a pile of rubble now?" Dolan asked in a more reasonable tone of voice.

Patrick stuffed his hands into his pockets. "Everything's burnt to ash inside or water logged. It'll have to be gutted."

Sandy breathed a great sigh of relief when the brothers momentarily settled down. The last thing he needed to deal with was explaining a battle royale to the McCormick's parents.

Sandy scanned Patrick's brother from head to toe, giving him the once over for the first time. Despite the spendy suit, he didn't look like a criminal. In his imagination, Dolan wore shiny suits, slicked back his hair, and smoked cigars like a character on *The Sopranos*. This guy looked more like a run-of-the-mill Chicago businessman—useless and boring.

"I'm going back in." Dolan threw a thumb in the direction of the hospital room.

Sandy reached out for Patrick before he followed. "So, what do you think?"

"I'm going to call the sheriff now." As Patrick pulled his phone out of his pocket, a woman stepped out of Pat's room.

Sandy stepped back, instantly recognizing her as the Lance Right Corporation HR representative. He held his breath. *Please don't recognize me. She didn't the other day, so chances are she won't recall my face now either, right?* He folded his arms and then unfolded them, failing in his attempt to appear relaxed and not nervous.

She held her hand out to Patrick. "We briefly met the other night at the store. I'm Nancy with the Lance Right Corporation. I wanted to check on your father." She handed Patrick her card and then turned to shake Sandy's hand.

Sandy gave her a tight smile.

She continued shaking his hand as her brows came together. "Sorry, but your face is familiar."

Sandy shrugged.

"Don't worry. We're not going to sue." The accusal in Patrick's flat words intruded on the attention she'd focused on Sandy.

"Oh no, that's not why I'm here." Her voice rose to a shrill pitch and her hand fluttered in front of her like a wounded butterfly. "Well, you have my number, please call me if there's anything that we can do for your family." She gave a nod and walked away.

But before she got too far, Patrick tapped her on her shoulder. "There's something you can do. I have an employee I think would be terrific manager material for your store."

"Wonderful, email me their resume. I'm sure with your endorsement they'd be an excellent addition to our team." She turned, paused, and snapped her fingers in the air. "I know who you are—Sandy Holiday—you're our new product placement photographer. That would have bothered me all day." Nancy's phone buzzed. She checked it and gave a wave. "Nice seeing you again." Nancy walked away.

Once she was around the corner, Patrick turned to Sandy, his face red. "Tell me what she's talking about."

Sandy clasped his hands together until they blanched. "This is what I was going to talk to you about. I'm . . . I have a job with them beginning next year."

"What the fuck?"

"I planned to tell you earlier, but then when I found out that they were, are, your arch enemy and direct competitor out to ruin your business . . . I decided to wait."

"Wow." Patrick's features twisted in disgust. "This entire time you had this job, and you didn't say squat?"

"I needed the job. The one at your store. And I need the one with them. You're not the only human being in town with financial problems."

Patrick's head shot back as if Sandy had jabbed his chin. "That's low. You show up and change everything and then what were you planning? Just bail and leave us once the new year rolled around? How could you even consider this?"

"I'm a photographer. I accepted the contract with them before I even knew you. I have to go where the money is to support myself. How the fuck don't you get it? Look at your store. You were one step away from bankruptcy. You're just fortunate that it burned down so you can collect on the insurance money."

Patrick's arms dropped by his sides. "Get the fuck out of my sight."

"Shit. I didn't mean that." Sandy stepped toward him.

Patrick put his hands up. "Don't touch me. I want you out of my house. I want you out of my town."

"It's not like you trusted me anyway, is it? How could you, though? With your brother screwing you over it was only a matter of time before I did."

"Yeah, and you proved me correct. And don't act like you didn't have one foot out the door the entire time we were getting close—tanking our date. I should have known you weren't ready. This is why you don't have a partner. You're not worth it." Patrick stormed off.

Sandy's hand pressed against his chest as he struggled to breathe. Swallowing his emotions, he needed to get away from Patrick. He needed an open space—preferably someplace that had a lot of oxygen. His walk turned into a jog, and then he was flat out running. He hated running, but he hated being this close to Patrick more. As the electric doors swooshed open, Sandy turned and kept going. His jacket flapped in the wind behind him as he ran across the parking lot.

He didn't know what he was doing or where he was going, but he didn't care. His lungs burned. He wasn't a runner. He hated exercise of all forms, but right now he hated Patrick more. He hated his crooked nose, his perfect torso, and that damn shaggy hair. But most of all, he hated that stupid lumberjack-looking beard and his dumb affinity for all things flannel.

As he ran across the viaduct over the highway, rain started to pelt him in the face and his legs were ready to give out. He turned toward a fast-food restaurant and slowed to a walk. With his head down, he pushed inside to nab some napkins and dry off his face and neck. Distraught and exhausted as he was, the grease from the grill managed to catch his attention. The magnet scent pulled his feet up to the counter where he ordered his weight in burgers, nuggets, onion rings, and, to top it all off, a giant chocolate shake. While he waited for his order, he shook out his coat and claimed a booth. He slid into the vinyl seat by the window. The rain started to come down in sheets. He sighed; the gray morning sky mirrored his feelings. He didn't have his car. *What's the plan? Walk down the highway? I might deserve that, but my leather shoes don't.* No, that's not an option. He pulled his cell out of his jacket and texted Chelsea. If they couldn't pick him up then he might have to hitchhike, which might force him into a situation where he'd have to listen to conservative talk radio. He shuddered at that horrible torture.

Thankfully, Chelsea agreed to chauffeur his ass back to Mayfield and his car, no questions asked.

As three trays of food appeared at his table, he stared blankly. He snatched some napkins to blot the water that overflowed from his eyes. He didn't know where the hell this inconvenient emotion was coming from or why. He'd only known Patrick for a handful of days. *No man is worth this shit.* He tossed his used napkins on the tray and unwrapped one of the burgers. "Hello, my love." He bit into it, hoping the quarter-pounder could fill the void inside of him like it usually did.

Six burgers, some nuggets, and several boxes of onion rings later, Chelsea pulled into a spot directly outside of his booth. He tidied up his table, crumpling the greasy paper into balls and stacking his trays. He sucked on his shake as Chelsea stopped at the counter for only a coffee. *Ugh, now I feel guilty. Couldn't they at least get some fries or something?*

Chelsea slid into the seat opposite him, cupping their hands around the large coffee.

"I didn't know who else to call for help." Sandy couldn't meet their eyes. He slurped from his shake and debated getting a third one. *The peppermint one looks good. Maybe if I drink that I'll explode and won't have to deal with whatever is breaking inside of me.*

Chelsea didn't move, didn't blink. Sandy wondered if their breathing had stopped. Their immobility cracked through all his barriers.

"I screwed up. I lied to him, and now he hates me and never wants to see me again. He's banished me from town, but who could blame him? I deserve to be sent to that stinking tiny island for misfit toys," he confessed with closed eyes as he set the empty shake cup on the table.

"Don't knock the island of misfit toys."

He opened his eyelids. Their deadpan expression didn't flinch.

"That's all you have to say?"

They took a sip of their coffee. "His Irish temper runs hot. Give him time to cool off."

Sandy threw a hand in their face, making a circle. "I liked it better when you didn't speak."

Chelsea smirked. They gave him a head nod as they slid out of the booth.

Sandy shrugged his jacket over his shoulders. As he dumped his garbage and trays, he truly hoped Chelsea was correct and that Patrick just needed time. But for some strange reason, it didn't feel like he would.

Chelsea waited for him by the door.

"Give me a minute." He held a finger in the air and then stopped by the counter. "The largest of the largest of your peppermint shake, please." May as well try to drown his sorrows in a vat of Christmassy goodness.

———

Slouching in a chair in the hospital lobby, Patrick stared at his phone. He'd called the sheriff, the insurance company, the bank, and all the other people he was required to contact.

And now he wanted to shrink into a little ball of misery and roll away.

Disappointment and failure clung to him like the stench of burned Christmas cookies. He needed to get up. He needed to go sit with his family, but his butt stayed in the chair, wallowing in self-pity. Of course, the last person he wanted to talk to sat down next to him. Well, maybe not the very last, but the second to last anyway.

"Been looking for you." Dolan glanced at him. "Dad's sleeping. You look like shit."

"Thanks. That's exactly what I needed to hear." He shook his head with disgust.

His ne'er-do-well brother started to stand, but hesitated. "Do you—" He cleared his throat. "I mean, do you need anything?"

That question threw Patrick off completely. His brother didn't willingly ever do anything out of the goodness of his heart because he didn't have one. He was worse than the Grinch and Scrooge combined. The only thing he could count on Dolan to do was to push him over a cliff like the Abominable Snowman, but there'd be no bouncing back to life for him. His features distorted at the mere suggestion that Dolan could deliver anything other than stolen goods.

His brother held his hands up. "All I'm saying is that you're not alone in all of this."

Patrick rolled his eyes. *If one more person says this to me, I'll beat them with something a whole lot more brutal than a candy cane.*

"Did it, again, somehow, didn't I?" Dolan shook his head.

"I'm never going to say the right thing, am I? Although, does anyone with you? It's only a store."

"You would say that. Do you have any idea how much of my life was put into it?"

"Yeah, I do and it's idiotic. As far as what Mom tells me, you weren't living. For years you've been dedicating yourself to only work, pushing relationships aside. The last guy you were with left you cuz of it. Then this other guy comes along when you need him the most, and you finally get a chance to have something more in your life and what . . . you throw him away because you lost your job?"

He shook his head, irritated. "You don't know what you're talking about."

"Enlighten me."

"I can't trust him."

Dolan scoffed as if that was the most absurd thing he'd ever heard. "There's a difference between not wanting to trust someone because you've been burned before, which is you, and not trusting someone because they're no good. But, if you ask me, people evolve, so that kind of doesn't matter anyway."

"Why am I talking to you?" Patrick growled.

"Because even though I screwed up and broke your trust, you're still talking to me and you're still trusting me, too."

Patrick glared at him as if he'd gone completely crazy.

"I didn't give you any proof of my innocence; you took my word and talked to the sheriff on my behalf." Dolan spread a palm out as if visually laying his point before Patrick's feet.

"He'll do the leg work and bust your ass if you're guilty."
Patrick looked away. *And I feel like a dumbass for doing that.*

The crooked smile Dolan gave him reminded him of when
they were kids and giving one another a hard time. "Mom
said you like this guy. Maybe it's time to give someone else
the benefit of the doubt? Where'd he go?"

Now I feel foolish. "Back to Chicago. Who knows?" It really
didn't matter where the adorable goof had gone. He wasn't
hoping Sandy would come back. No, he was glad to be rid of
him. They were a mismatch. A stupid holiday mistake that
ended before it even began. Plus, he had other things to
worry about, right?

"Do you know when I knew I wanted to marry Emily?"

Patrick refused to look at his brother. He didn't want to
listen to some sappy story about his undeserving brother
falling in love.

"I told her about taking the money, and she made me call
Mom and Dad and apologize and send them the money I
stole."

Stunned, Patrick whipped his head around, gaping at
Dolan. His parents never told him about any of this, especially the part about him returning all the cash. *What happened
to the money? They had to have reinvested it in the Madison store.*

"They didn't tell you because I asked them not to. You've
had a lot on your plate because of what I did for years, and I
didn't want to stir things up for you again." Dolan leaned his
elbows on his knees. "Emily accepted me for who I was and
for who I became. Even the crappiest version of myself, she
loved me, flaws and all."

"Are you saying I should forgive Sandy for all of his flaws?"

Dolan shook his head. "I'm saying forgive yourself first because you're blaming him for all of it, but you gotta see that you had a part in it too."

Baffled at this sudden depth coming from his brother, he stared at him. This unexpected wisdom seemed like a trick.

Dolan stood. "Gonna find some coffee. You want any?"

This revealing conversation had left him numb. Patrick shook his head.

"See you back at Dad's room, yeah?" Dolan patted Patrick's shoulder.

There's a slim chance that he's right. How can I be pissed at Sandy for taking a job with Lance Right when I'm submitting Chelsea for a managerial position with them? The difference was that Sandy knew from the very beginning and had purposely kept the information secret. Patrick dropped his head against the back of the chair. This was torture. And he hated to admit it, but he really missed Sandy.

CHAPTER 17

With Chelsea's help, Sandy gathered his things and packed his Prius. Before leaving Mayfield, he told them everything that led to the break up. They said to give it time, but Sandy was never very good at the waiting game. As he drove down the highway back to Chicago, he couldn't prevent his lips from pouting. Not only had he lost his holiday gig, but he'd lost a guy he genuinely connected with beyond a physical relationship, which was a first. All his emotions hit him at once, and he realized he didn't want to be alone. But Julia was out of town, and he wasn't in the mood to go out to any of the bars. He surprised himself when he hit the FaceTime icon to call his mom.

"You're not dying and you're FaceTiming? Are you sure you're not ill? You should not do the FaceTime while driving." His mom brought the phone close to her face so she could look at him.

"Don't worry. I have a holder on the dash."

Harley pulled the phone back, so he and his mom both appeared on screen. "That may be, son, but we're only thinking of your safety."

Sandy refrained from rolling his eyes, but it took great strength.

"Is everything all right?" His mom pushed her glasses up her nose.

"Fine. It's fine. I'm fine." He inhaled, trying not to get worked up. "I wanted to see if you'd like to have dinner."

"Heck yeah, we do. Come on over. I got some pork going in the oven." Harley beamed brighter than Rudolph's nose. He was the most excitable person on the face of the earth.

"And we have plenty of miso soup."

He hated to admit it, but all of that sounded perfect. "I'm coming straight to yours."

"Whoo-hoo. I'm gonna get the bourbon out. We're having cocktails." Harley slapped the counter.

"You better drive quick, otherwise he will start without you," she mumbled close to the phone.

"I heard that. You're gonna like this one, my boy." Harley hooted enthusiastically.

Mom shook her head, but Sandy knew she enjoyed her husband's wild outbursts.

"See you soon." Sandy ended the call. Somehow that call made his spirits lift even if it was a minimal amount. In a way, he needed to be with them tonight. He needed them to play the love-smothering couple and make him eat too much and drink too much. And perhaps he even needed them to talk him into staying overnight in his old bedroom. *Ugh, what is wrong with me?* Moonshine nudged her nose into his arm. "Why didn't you have the sense to talk me out of this?"

———

Forty-five minutes later, Sandy pulled into the drive at his parents' Forest Glen home. Contrary to many of the other homes in that area, his parents owned a modest four-bedroom, three-bathroom, two-story home. His mom filled it with tchotchkes, and she preserved his teenage room with Britney Spears posters.

Before Sandy could say a word, his mother shouted greetings from the door and his stepfather had bounded out of the house and taken out Sandy's bags. "I don't know if I'm staying."

"We're having cocktails. You're staying," Harley responded.

Sandy grabbed Moonshine's leash and followed Harley up the steps, and stopped to kiss his mom on the cheek. The home always smelled the same, a mixture of his mom's cooking and Harley's woodworking projects. Tonight, the savory scent of miso soup welcomed him.

Harley trudged up the stairs.

"He doesn't have to do this." Sandy unhooked Moonshine's leash. The dog barked and headed toward the kitchen, probably enroute to the doggie door his parents still had, even though it was years since their old beagle Bubba had gotten his wings.

"Let him. He likes to do stuff for you." His mom turned to him and poked his belly. "You're getting soft."

Sandy rolled his eyes as he took off his shoes. "Hey, I really don't need to be fat-shamed right now."

"I'm not shaming you. I'm telling you that you have a pouch. Come." Mom followed Sandy and stopped in the kitchen.

He shook his head at his mom's unique way of twisting his words.

Harley rounded the corner and patted Sandy's shoulders. "This is gonna knock your socks off." His stepdad had a bunch of items and glasses out to mix their cocktails. "Got this bourbon straight from a small batch distillery in Tennessee."

Sandy took a seat at the kitchen island. He could really use a drink.

"Why does your face look all frowny?" Annie stood across from him as she started placing pickled carrots and onions in a bowl.

"Long day. Long drive. Long everything." Sandy blew his bangs out of his eyes and headed to the back door. He grabbed a towel to dry off Moonshine.

"I don't believe you." His mom raised her voice.

"She doesn't believe me. Shocking," he said to Moonshine before rejoining his parents. Harley handed him his drink, and he took a big swig. The ginger hit the back of his throat, and he covered his mouth, choking the liquid back down. "Nutcrackers!"

"Yeah, it's got a kick. I call it Ginger Snapped." Harley's features lit up with pride.

"More like Ginger Bitch-Slaps. Wow. This is potent. I love it." Sandy patted his stepdad on the arm.

His mom rounded the island and headed into the cozy living room, where a fire was blazing away in the fireplace. She held a mug of tea in one hand and a bowl of mixed nuts in the other. Sandy followed her and took a seat on the floor, where there were half a million pillows for sitting. "You have too many pillows. This is ridiculous."

Harley moved a bunch of pillows on the couch, too, and sat down. He threw his arm behind Mom. There was barely an inch between the two. "He's avoiding something big," Harley mumbled to her.

Sandy threw a pillow at Harley, who caught it and placed it in his lap. "You gotta be quicker on the draw than that."

"Why are you here? What happened to the nice boy?" His mom reached for the nuts on the coffee table and took a handful, sharing with Harley.

How does she do this?

"You're sulking like when that boy in fourth grade broke your heart. Remember him?" She glanced up at Harley.

Harley took a sip of his drink, wrinkling his features in thought. "That scrawny kid."

"With the hair." She lifted her hand above her head, indicating the messy style Dennis Parks' messy hair style. Not that Sandy remembered his name or his favorite color or the fact that last year he'd liked one of Sandy's tweets and then Sandy proceeded to stalk him online only to find out that he was happily married to a man who looked exactly like him and their 2.5 children.

"Can we please stop skipping down memory lane?" Sandy smiled, enjoying this even though he'd never admit it. *I'm just going to tell them, because that's why I'm here, isn't it?* "Before anymore guessing ensues, I made a mistake with Patrick and things . . . dissolved."

His mom silently stared at him as she blew on her tea.

Harley stirred his drink.

"What did you do? Why do you push everyone away from you? You're handsome, talented, and you think you're very funny. Why do you do this to yourself?" Mom rattled off as she set her mug down.

Sandy pointed a finger at himself. "Me? I'm the problem?" He looked between his mom and stepdad, baffled by that announcement. Harley had gone oddly silent and averted his eyes. "I don't believe this." He slapped a pillow to emphasize his indignation.

Moonshine sat next to him and sneezed as if on Harley and Mom's side.

"You don't get a vote."

The dog barked and turned away, hopping up on the couch next to mom and curling into a ball as if offended by Sandy's dismissal.

Harley cleared his throat. "Perhaps what it comes down to is that you might get in your own way."

Sandy inhaled. He couldn't deny that he did block his own way to happiness with Patrick. He could have been upfront about his new job. But it was too late, wasn't it?

His mom tilted her head at him. "You like him."

Sandy lifted a shoulder, acting indifferent.

"You want to get him back." His mom pointed at him. "You came to us for help!" She sat up and practically wiggled in her seat.

"Ha. No. Not at all. That's a big glass of never ever." Sandy hid behind his cocktail and took a long sip. *Oh yeah, I'm having another if I'm going to drown out all her excitement. Why did Julia have to go to Japan? She's so selfish.*

"I got an idea." With big eyes, Harley glanced between his mom and Sandy. "What you need is a grand idea like a big, in his face, I-like-you bouquet."

Mom tsked. "Not flowers. That's not good enough. Bigger."

"Bigger?" Harley rubbed his chin as if he were Santa about to fire up the sleigh to get his gift. "What's he into?"

"Until recently he lived for his job, but they lost the store in a fire, so now he's starting over from scratch."

"That's work. What about outside of all that?" Harley rattled the ice and leftover liquid in his glass.

"Sadly, that's been his life for so long it's the only thing he's been living for, well, and his obsessive need to exercise. He might want to get into coaching." Sandy stirred his empty glass, considering what could help Patrick the most. "They have a lot of bills to pay off."

Harley stood and took his empty glass to the kitchen. "I'm turning off the soup."

Mom waved a hand in the air. "Then help him raise money."

Sandy bobbed his head. The fundraiser page was still up, and he'd have to check that later. "Don't I need something more personal?"

Harley sat back down. "How about a silent auction?"

She patted his knee at the idea. "I can make finger food."

Sandy gazed at the flames dancing in the fireplace, considering the scope of all of this and how he could even afford to do something like it in a short time span.

"Have it at the Asian American Community Center, and you can auction off your photos."

"I got a Rolodex full of clients and other docs and dentists that we can easily nudge into spending their money." Harley said.

"You're showing your age using that old timey language." Sandy smirked into his cocktail glass. "But if you're making these Ginger Bitches for them, their money will fly outta their pockets. This is all absurd, isn't it? How am I going to get all this together before Christmas?"

"We'll use the center's phone tree and Harley's Rolodex from the 1980s." Mom winked at Sandy. "And call the gays."

Sandy shook his head at his mom. In her mind it was really this simple. If only he was this positive. But he had to try, didn't he? If he was serious about Patrick and his feelings for him, then he couldn't stop at anything to try to win him back. "Ok, let's do this thing."

———

Patrick was lying in bed, staring at the ceiling. He hadn't slept at all last night. Every single time he turned in bed he expected Sandy to be there snoring next to him. How had he gotten so used to the man invading his space so fast? Patrick kicked the covers off.

He pulled on a sweatshirt and changed from pajama bottoms to jeans. Instead of making breakfast, he'd walk to Viv's and pick up some pastries. And he hoped the morning air would invigorate him. He needed the cold to slap him out of his thoughts.

As he tied his boots and put on the rest of his winter gear, he even missed the morning routine with Sandy. He missed seeing his shoes mixed in with his own. He missed the preppy jacket Sandy wore and his inability to dress properly in winter weather. *How did he survive in Chicago?*

Big fluffy flakes of snow fell as Patrick traveled through the park and toward the café. The way Sandy's face lit up when they walked this route on that first night was something he'd never forget. And their playful snowball fight had made Patrick recognize right away that this man was something special. His stomach dropped at the idea of never goofing off with Sandy ever again.

When he arrived at Viv's, the café was bustling with regulars. He moved to the pastry display, where Viv slid a fresh tray of chocolate croissants into the case. He requested four and ordered a coffee to go.

Chelsea stopped next to him with their hunched gait, removing their gloves.

"Did you come down the chimney?" Patrick smiled at the arrival of his friend.

They nodded and gave him a sly look as if maybe they did wear Santa's red suit. "Thanks for the recommendation. Made Mom's day that I got a new job already."

"Happy to help." Patrick took his coffee from Viv. They gravitated to the counter and sat down.

Chelsea dipped their head down. "Hey, um, not sure if you heard, but they arrested Wayne."

Surprised, Patrick leaned back in his chair. He hadn't been expecting that news at all. "Are they sure it was him?"

"Found the same gas cans at his place and other stuff. Evidence. When they picked him up, he was passed out drunk at his front door. He got frostbite."

Patrick rubbed a palm across his face. What a terrible ending for Wayne and the store. "He needs help." He'd make a call to the sheriff today. Maybe he could speak on his behalf and get him into rehab.

"Haven't seen Sandy around . . . " Chelsea glanced at him and then away as if the idea of talking about relationships made them uncomfortable.

Patrick averted his eyes. Instead of discussing his personal life, he sipped his coffee.

Chelsea removed their phone from their pocket and hit a few buttons. They slid it over to Patrick to see the screen. "The store GoFundMe page blew up last night."

He took a quick peek at the screen, then grabbed the phone in shock. "This is . . . this is incredible." The funds raised could pay off the debt that they owed. The urge to text

Sandy crossed his mind, but he couldn't do that. *What would I say? And he probably doesn't want to talk to me anyway.*

"Not enough to cover rebuilding, but it's a good start." Chelsea took their phone back. "What are your plans now?"

Uncertainty coursed through him. "I don't have a clue. I'll have to discuss this with my parents. It's up to them if they want to start over with another store, but I'm thinking I need to move in a new direction."

Chelsea slipped on their gloves and took a takeout bag from Viv. "Whatever you do will be great. Glad you're braving a new path. It's scary as fuck, but you can do it."

Patrick glanced up at them. "Did you just give me a pep talk?"

Chelsea gave him a one-armed shrug. "No idea what you're going on about." They turned and headed for the back exit.

He chuckled as a smile crept across his mouth.

CHAPTER 18

That afternoon, Patrick dropped into a chair next to his dad's bedside. His mom and Dolan sat on the opposite side. His dad's color had returned, and the doctor was optimistic about his blood pressure and workup, which was more than Patrick could have hoped for this Christmas. He didn't plan to upset his parents, but they needed to discuss the store's future.

"Dad, are you up for a talk about the business?" he asked as gently as possible.

Dad nodded and sipped from his water cup.

Dolan stood. "I'll just go—"

"Stay." Patrick raised a hand. "You should be here for this."

His brother glanced at the faces all around him. He drew in a breath and sat back down.

Patrick cleared his throat. "We need to discuss the Mayfield store."

"Your mom told me about the fire. I'm happy no one was hurt." His dad patted Patrick's hand.

Patrick was elated he didn't have to have that conversation along with his own news. "Same here. But I don't think we should rebuild the Mayfield store. It's time to let it go."

His dad glanced between Patrick and mom.

"And I'm not going to be a part of the business anymore."

His dad struggled to sit up, flustered when the pillows didn't mold to his shuffling. Patrick stood and helped as his mom moved the pillows.

"You can't run away after one incident. That's not how this works." His dad's voice rose with displeasure.

"That's not what I'm doing. I need to branch out and try something new. Something that doesn't suck the life out of me and demand every single second of my attention. Maybe coaching?"

His dad shot mom a glare. "Did you know about this?"

"Calm down." She inhaled as if to trying to get him to breathe with her. "I didn't, but I think it's a grand idea. It's time. And since you're in no position to run off to the store, this is a fine time to circle back around to your retirement."

Dad scoffed like it was the most absurd thing he'd heard all day. "Don't be ridiculous."

Mom sat on the edge of the bed. "Here's what will happen. Eric will manage the Madison store for the next couple of months until we either sell or go out of business; either way the business will close."

"I can help with that," Dolan volunteered. "And that way Patrick can transition into something new, and Dad can continue to recuperate."

Dad shook his head. "It's too soon. It's the recession and inflation. We've hit a slump is all."

"That's not true," Patrick said. "The Mayfield branch has been struggling for over a year. Even with the updates we've made it would take a lot more to dig us out of the hole we're in. The GoFundMe page will help a little, but not much."

His dad inhaled as if on the verge of protesting.

Before his dad could say anything, Patrick continued. "Yes, I ignored your orders to bring the page down. I think we should go out of business gracefully and on our own terms. This will be hard. The stores have meant so much to us over the years. I'm glad I got to be a part of something so amazing." Patrick squeezed his dad's hand hoping to convey how much he loved working with his dad.

"We've had a good run." Dad looked at mom with a kind of half-smile on his face.

"Survived the internet and big competition for years." She kissed his hand.

Patrick looked from one parent to the next. He wanted that, a partnership. His parents always balanced one another perfectly. *Will I ever have this kind of relationship?*

"Call Eric. Let him know—"

Mom cut him off. "Don't worry. I know exactly what to say. I'm proud of you." She gave him a kiss before she stepped out to make the call.

"I'm gonna pop out, too, and check in with Emily." Dolan headed for the door.

"So . . . what happened to Sandy? I thought I'd see him today. Is he afraid a panic attack and high blood pressure is catchy?" Dad guffawed at his own lame joke.

"He went home." Patrick shifted in his chair, uncomfortable with the idea of discussing his failed relationship with Sandy.

"When's he coming back?"

Patrick averted his eyes.

"Listen, I know you're not comfortable talking to me about your boyfriends and that you'd rather talk to your mom about it, but I'd really like us to talk more."

Patrick's jaw practically hit the floor. "What? I always thought you were the one who didn't want to know about my relationships."

"Did I ever say that?"

"You never didn't not say it."

Dad squinted at him, his brows furrowed. "Not sure I got all that, but you never came to me."

Patrick shook his head. "I did. I know I did." He tried to recall a time when he sought out his dad to discuss the men he dated.

"Once when you were in college, otherwise you bypassed me."

"Yeah, and you got weird. Really quiet, which freaked me out."

Dad shrugged. "I was trying to listen."

Patrick placed his hands over his face. After all these

years, the truth had finally come out, and it was that his dad had been trying to be a good dad. He wished he could kick himself in the ass.

"You and Sandy worked well together. Even saved my life together. You sure there's not something there that you're going to miss?"

"He lied to me."

His dad waved a hand in the air like that didn't matter. "You think I never lied to your mother? Only problem is that now she knows all my tells, so it's impossible to do anymore. You talk about trying something new in your career, then why can't you do that with this guy? Try something new, try trusting that he won't lie to you again."

"But what if he does?"

"You gotta cross that bridge when you get to it. Decide if his dishonesty is a mistake or a habit. Do you think I wanted to forgive your brother? I didn't want to, but I love him. Sure, your mom pushed me some, too. I won't do that to you. You're not there yet with Dolan and the forgiveness—I understand that. It's okay. That kind of broken trust does something to a person. He's part of our family. But with your guy it could be something more if you give him another chance. Ya know I could be wrong, but I think you love Sandy, and that's why it's eating you up. Question is, are you going to let him go or do something about it?"

My dad is secretly Dumbledore. When the hell did this happen? Maybe I should have come to him years ago for relationship advice. Patrick sat there allowing the words to soak into him like alcohol in a rum ball, the wisdom just as potent as the booze in those decadent holiday treats. No, he wasn't ready to forgive Sandy, but he didn't want to give up.

"You goin' to Chicago or what?" his dad barked at him.

Patrick snapped out of it. "Yeah, I think I'm up for a challenge."

"Attaboy." Dad leaned forward and smacked his upper arm just like he'd do before Patrick's wrestling matches.

Suddenly, he was fired up. Patrick gathered his jacket, and bent down to hug his dad. "Be good."

Dad roared with laughter. "I should say the same to you."

Patrick waved a hand in the air and headed out the door. *I don't think I've been this nervous since my first university match.* He blew out a huff of air and strode down the hall. His dad's nurse for the day rounded the corner and almost ran into him.

"Excuse me, Mr. McCormick. I was just about to head into your father's room. Did you hear there's an emergency services alert for a winter storm?"

Patrick dug his phone out of his pocket, but he had it on do not disturb and missed all the alert notifications. "Son of a reindeer."

———

Sandy spent the next three snowbound days at Julia's townhouse. It was the worst storm in the Chicago area in decades. Thankfully, he hadn't gotten stuck at his parents' place. One night was more than enough, thank you very much, although, he had been constantly on the phone with them coordinating the details for the silent auction. His eyes burned from staring at the list of silent auction items his mom just emailed to him while working on cutting a new mat for another one of his black and white portraits. He was sitting on the floor with the mat between his legs, squinting at the laptop on the coffee table. The auction was turning into a larger affair that he'd dreamed.

"Please tell me I still have some cookies left," Sandy said to Moonshine as he climbed to his feet in search of sugar.

Moonshine barked as if telling Sandy that he shouldn't eat anymore.

"Hey, no nagging, no shaming. If I want to drown my frustrations in a pound of pure cane sugar then I'm damn well going to."

The dog sneezed in disagreement.

"You don't get a vote." Sandy popped the top on the Tupperware container where his gingerbread men were stored. He shoved one in his mouth as he slid over to the refrigerator to retrieve a carton of eggnog before searching the cupboards for a bottle of whiskey. As he whipped up his holiday cocktail, his phone buzzed from the counter. His mom's face filled the screen. He added another shot of whiskey for good measure before hitting the FaceTime button.

"Did you get the email?" His mom threw etiquette out the window when a new project was on the line. And thanks to Sandy's own big mouth, his love life was her new pet project.

Sandy held a finger in the air, asking her to hold on as he

took a few gulps of his drink. He took a bite of cookie and chewed. "That's a lot of junk to auction off, Ma."

"Too much sugar. Stop eating and drinking or you'll look like Santa by the time he sees you. Check your computer. I sent the contract to you to sign."

He balanced two cookies on top of his glass as he navigated his way back to his laptop. "What contract?

"Don't be dumb. For the Asian Community Center. The board needs a signed contract for insurance and liability purposes."

"Yeah, but don't you like run the board?"

"Doesn't matter. Shut up and sign." She pointed at the screen like he was signing a piece of paper.

He set everything on the coffee table and took a seat on the floor. He opened the email and scrolled through the document. "Wait a minute, this says we're having it in two days."

His mom didn't blink.

"Two days! Have you gone completely jingle bells? There's no way we can pull this together that quickly."

"Ah, but yes we can."

Harley's head popped over his mom's shoulder. "We have the magic of the phone tree."

Sandy stuffed an entire gingerbread man into his mouth and washed it down with half of his lit nog.

Mom clapped her hands loud enough that Moonshine woke up and barked. The combination almost shocked Sandy into a spit take.

He placed a hand over his mouth as he finished chewing. "Don't do that while I'm eating."

"He won't want you if you resemble a fat panda."

"You are a horrible, awful, elf of a woman."

"Sign the papers."

Sandy dropped in his DocuSign signature and hit complete. "Done. Now stop bothering me. I have work to do." He worried his bottom lip.

"What's wrong?"

"Nothing. I have a lot to do that's all."

"Your mom's right. What's eatin' ya, son?" Harley's brows met.

He gulped more nog. "Okay, what if he thinks I'm doing all this because I feel guilty and bad?"

"But you do."

"I like him and his family more, and I want to help them."

His mom and Harley did that collective sigh-and-gaze-at one-another that didn't bother him nearly as much as it used to. *I'm getting soft all right.* He dunked his second cookie into his cocktail and bit into it.

"Then tell him that when you see him," Harley replied, as if that was the most obvious answer, which it was. But Sandy feared it would come off as pressure, and that's the last thing he wished to do to Patrick.

"I'm sending out the email invites tonight." His mom slid that nugget into the conversation, blindsiding him.

"What?!" Cookie crumbs flew out of his mouth. A few stuck to the face of his phone. He set his cookie down. "I'm not ready."

"If you put the cookies down, you will be."

"Don't worry about a thing. You concentrate on what you

need to finish up for the auction. We got the rest for ya." Harley winked at him.

Sandy gave them a frantic wave goodbye and ended the call. He covered his face with his hands and reclined against the base of the couch. When he dropped his hands, he noticed his cookie had mysteriously gone missing. Moonshine was chomping away on the baked good. All that was left was a gingerbread leg, and that appendage disappeared in the next bite.

"You're on their team, aren't you?" Sandy sneered at the pooch.

Moonshine barked and wagged her tail.

"Fine. I'll get to work, you evil dog." Plus, working could take his mind off thinking of the words he needed to say to Patrick. But were words good enough at this point?

CHAPTER 19

Patrick paced in front of the doors of the Asian Community Center. This was what he'd been doing for the past ten minutes. Occasionally, he'd open the door for someone. Mostly, there was the pacing and his nervous muttering. The last time he was this anxious was when he was a kid at his first wrestling match. He barfed twice before hitting the mat. Part of him wished he'd taken his family and Chelsea up on their offers to come with him.

He stopped pacing. In the glass reflection of the windows, he adjusted his tie. His mom suggested he wear a suit, but he always managed to twist himself up inside formal attire. "You look ridiculous," he said to himself.

"Green is your color," a teeny tiny Asian woman said from around the corner of the door. Her red and gold blouse sparkled in the moonlight as she greeted more attendees, saying hello and chatting up people as they arrived.

He glanced down at his Dartmouth green three-piece slim fit suit. The camel-color tie and matching handkerchief made him look like an Etsy model. *Am I trying too hard?*

"Would you like to come in?" She gave him what he'd call a sneaky smile.

Oh geez, even she knows I'm trying too hard. I should go.

She pulled him in by the elbow. "You look like you like spicy chicken wings. I made them. I'm Annie and they're oven baked. You must try some and tell me if they're good."

"I am kinda hungry." Patrick didn't mean to say that aloud, but Annie was too kind to resist.

"And gamjajeon."

"What's that?"

"A Korean potato pancake. You'll like it."

Before Patrick could blink, they were inside the community center. A band played holiday music from a stage, and decorated trees stood in each of the corners. Garlands of pine and sparkling lights hung from the windows and walls. The atmosphere was cozy with the lights dimmed low against the red fabric draped about the room.

Annie patted his arm as she walked away. "I'll fix you a plate."

Patrick nodded as he turned around to walk, looking for Sandy. He checked his coat and gravitated to the silent auction display. Spa vacation packages, gourmet wine baskets, and ski trips to Aspen were all up for grabs. But what caught Patrick's attention wasn't on any of the tables. In a section beyond the goodie tables was a gallery display of black and white portraits. He recognized a couple of the photos from Sandy's portfolio. He stopped at the nameplate of the artist:

ABOUT THE ARTIST

SANDY HOLIDAY IS A LOCAL PHOTOGRAPHER. BORN AND RAISED IN CHICAGO, SANDY SPECIALIZES IN BLACK AND WHITE PORTRAITS.

"I WANT MY PHOTOS TO TELL A STORY. WHEN YOU LOOK AT THEM, I WANT YOU TO GO ON THAT JOURNEY WITH THEM IN THAT MOMENT."

HE HAS TAKEN COMMERCIAL AND PRODUCT PHOTOS FOR BOUND BOOKS, HOLIDAY SPORTS MEDICINE, PURPLE MACHINE, BUCK'S BEER, AND WILDE'S WATERING HOLE. SANDY IS A MEMBER OF THE CHICAGO LGBTQIA+ CHAMBER OF COMMERCE.

The serious expression on Sandy's self-portrait photo was odd. Patrick never associated the word 'somber with Sandy's lively presence. Prying himself away from the professional face of the man he desperately wanted to see, Patrick strolled to the first piece. It was a series of three photos of an ancient, wrinkled man, eating a meatball, spilling the ball on himself, and ultimately laughing about it. Now this is what he expected from Sandy's sense of humor. As he moved along, each photo reminded him so much of Sandy's laughter, kindness, and joy. He stopped at a photo of Annie, who was near the water, laughing. Patrick glanced at the title card with the word MA written on it. The woman who'd met him at the door was Sandy's mom, which made perfect sense.

"I hoped you'd make it," a strained voice said from behind Patrick.

Patrick wiped his sweaty palms o his pants legs and turned.

And there he was, Sandy in a red vest, matching tie, and white shirt. His black floppy bangs hid part of his face, but there was a shy smile there, hidden until he finally looked up, meeting Patrick's eyes.

"People are going to think we planned this." Patrick moved his hand from his suit to Sandy's, indicating the green and red theme of their clothes.

"I won't mind, if you don't." Sandy took a few steps closer to Patrick.

"Here you are." Annie held a full plate out to Patrick with a roll of utensils.

"You two met?" Sandy's eyes traveled from his mom to Patrick.

"Of course." His mom kissed his cheek. "Go get drinks. I got things to do." And Annie was off just as quickly as she arrived.

Sandy blew his bangs out of his eyes. "How about you find a table for that gigantic plate of food, and I'll get the drinks?"

Patrick headed toward the main area in search of a place to sit. Everyone had the same idea. The only table left was in the center of the room, closest to the dance floor. He still couldn't believe what he was looking at: the people, the beautiful decorations, and the auction. It was all perfect, in fact.

Sandy took a seat across from Patrick and slid over a beer to him.

"This is a lot." Patrick circled his fork in the air, encompassing everything in the room. "How did you manage this?"

Sandy glanced around like he was noticing everything for the first time. "A Rolodex from the 1980s and my mom. She would have made a helluva dictator." Sandy cleared his throat. "I want to apologize for keeping my job a secret, but I don't want you to think that this has anything to do with that. It doesn't."

"No?" Patrick leaned forward on his elbows, curious where this was going.

"This event is about your family and the business. I need to help because I care about all of you, but I don't want to pressure you about us. Does this make sense?"

Patrick understood, and he appreciated the sentiment. "You really didn't have to do this."

"I did. And oh sweet gingerbread men, someone gave my mom a microphone." Sandy stood, holding a finger in the air. "Be right back."

"Ladies and gentlemen and non-binary friends . . . " Annie stood on the stage, squinting into the bright lights. "Can we dim this?"

Sandy swooped in next to his mom and slipped the mic out of her hands.

"Don't forget to project from your diaphragm," she suggested. The microphone still caught every word she uttered.

"I have a microphone and an amp. Do I really need to?"

"Sometimes you mumble."

"What? Never."

"Debate team. Sixth grade. You got a D." The boisterous laughter from the crowd filled the air.

Sandy placed a hand over his eyes. "On that note, the silent auction will begin momentarily. All proceeds from this evening's event will go to the McCormick Family and the Children's Health & Dental Clinic. Please enjoy your night, and don't forget to tip the band because they're playing for free."

"Ask him to dance." Annie's voice was still being caught by the microphone.

"Ma, you're pushing."

"All good romances need a push," she shouted as a version of "Christmas Baby Please Come Home" started up. Sandy left the stage, rejoining Patrick at the table.

"You're probably wondering about the Children's Clinic. My step pop is a sports doc, and since we basically broke his Rolodex to get people to come out for this event, we did a combination of sorts."

Overwhelmed with the love at this display of Sandy's kindness and generosity, but mostly with the need to get his hands on him after so many days apart, Patrick wiped a napkin across his mouth. "Do you want to dance?" He stood up and held out his hand.

Sandy's mouth opened, but no words emerged. Patrick took Sandy by the arm, encouraging him to stand with a tug.

He led them to the center of the dance floor. A few other couples joined in once they saw Patrick and Sandy. "This is amazing. Seriously, what you did here is impressive. And I'm glad the kids will benefit from this function. Honestly, they could take it all. With the insurance covering everything and your GoFundMe page, we really don't need much more to pay off the bills and shut down."

"No reopening in Mayfield?"

Patrick shook his head.

"What will you do? Move to Madison?"

"Nope, I'm out of the family business and Dad is set to retire—Mom made sure of that. I haven't a clue what I'm going to do next. It's a very uncomfortable feeling and nice at the same time." The song ended and they moved off the floor, heading to the silent auction. Patrick dipped his head down. "I owe you an apology. I overreacted about your job with Lance Right. It wasn't my place to tell you who you should work for, and nowadays, you can't give up a decent-paying job."

"Please—I should have said something. It's my fault entirely. I'm the one who's sorry. I hope I can earn your trust back in time."

Patrick stopped them at the display of Sandy's photos. "Look at these photos. You're so talented. I'm in awe of it. This one of your mom is incredible."

Sandy glanced at the photo. "Technically, that's supposed to be my Christmas gift to my mom. Don't tell her." Sandy's eyes widened at something over Patrick's shoulder.

Patrick turned around. A woman didn't realize it, but her wrap had gotten caught on a Christmas tree.

"Oh, holy night! Be right back before she topples the tree." Sandy ran toward the oblivious woman.

Patrick studied that amazing photo of Annie. He couldn't let Sandy lose his gift to her. Patrick dashed to the silent auction table. He located the clipboard for Sandy's photos and bid as high as he could go. Now wasn't the time to be spending his money, but he had enough saved from working nonstop over the years that he could splurge. And Sandy was worth everything. He scribbled two thousand dollars before rejoining Sandy at the saved Christmas tree.

The two worked together to rehang silver ornaments back on the branches.

A stray silver ball rolled next to Patrick's foot. He bent down to pick it up, then hung it on one of the limbs. "Saving trees and strangers . . . you're an exceptionally nice person," he said to Sandy as he adjusted a snowflake that looked on the verge of falling.

"Bite your tongue. Everyone knows I'm a snarky self-centered drama queen. Personally, I blame you for all your Wisconsin-nice rubbing off all over me and bringing out the best in me, which is legit annoying."

A devious smile stretched across Patrick's lips. "Rubbing off on you, huh?"

Sandy backhanded Patrick in the bicep. "Shut up."

He caught Sandy's hand and brought it to his chest. "I'm not saying this because of what you did here for my family . . . I like you. I want us to go on hikes, go to see a musical, and go camping."

"Fuck no. Did you name three things that I absolutely detest on purpose? How are we even compatible?"

Patrick dropped his hand and grabbed him around the neck, pulling him into a deep kiss. As the fire surged in Patrick's stomach and then to his cock, he knew they didn't need to do any of those things. And from the growly sound that Sandy made, he was onboard with whatever they did next.

Sandy pulled back from the kiss. "Want to get out of here?"

"You don't need to stay for the auction?"

"After that kiss? Are you for real? Ma can text me the highlights."

Perfect, because I already have several other activities in mind that we'll both enjoy.

———

Sandy couldn't stop smiling as Patrick pressed him into the front door of the Brownstone, ravishing his neck with kisses. Blindly, he fumbled the key, trying to shove it into the lock as Patrick's hands pushed open his jacket, rubbing them across his nipples. That combination did it for him. Patrick pushed against Sandy as if he was about to fuck him through his clothes. Finally, he twisted the lock home and got them into the foyer. He grabbed Patrick by the lapels and shoved his tongue down his throat, kicking the door shut with his foot and fumbling to flip the dead bolt closed.

Patrick peeled off his own jacket and then Sandy's. This

was one time Sandy didn't care about being tidy. He discarded his shoes and then stripped Patrick's suit coat off as he moved them in the direction of his bedroom. Once he got to the vest, he stopped. "Seriously, double breasted and eight zillion buttons? You couldn't find a corset?"

"They were all out." Patrick loosened Sandy's tie.

Sandy flipped on the standing light at the entrance of his bedroom and then started to unbutton his own vest. Patrick did the same with his.

"Before we do this, promise me I never have to do any of those things you listed. This body was not made to sit through three-hours of singing nor cavorting with bugs."

"What about volunteering? Or doing some travelling together. You could take pictures."

Sandy flung off his vest, shirt and pants and practically ran over to remove the rest of Patrick's clothes. "Done. I'll give until I can't give no more, and then I'll photograph you naked."

Patrick's fingers dug into Sandy's ass as he pulled him into him for a kiss. Sandy groaned as Patrick's hardness rubbed against him. He couldn't wait any longer to taste Patrick. Sandy went to his knees and pulled Patrick's fitted boxers down his legs. "Hold on, Santa, this is going to be a bumpy ride." He wrapped his mouth around Patrick's cock and grasped his ass.

———

There was ringing. Loud bells ringing. Loud, annoying bells ringing. Sandy wished whoever decided to bother him after he and Patrick spent the majority of the evening exploring each other's bodies would fall into a pile of snow. He rolled over onto his back, glancing at his bed mate, who was unfortunately covered by the duvet. Sandy sighed as he slipped into his pajamas and slippers and started down the stairs to the front door.

He could only assume the tiny figure on the welcome mat bundled under a hundred layers with a scarf around her face was his mom. Her eyes blinked and then her glasses fogged once she stepped inside the warm interior. Sandy swung the door shut for her, seeing as she was barely gripping a large, wrapped, rectangular box.

Mom knocked off her boots on the rug and held the box out to Sandy. He put it to the side to help her pull her scarf away from her mouth for her to speak. "Good morning."

Sandy pulled off her foggy eyewear and wagged them in the air to clear the cloudiness. "What are you doing here and why at the crack of dawn?"

"It's seven in the morning. Why are you still in bed?" She took her glasses back and placed them on her nose.

Patrick came down the stairs, tying the drawstring on what looked like a pair of Julia's old sweatpants. The pants were tight and short. Sandy's eyes bugged out once he glimpsed the visible bulge between Patrick's legs. He quickly grabbed Patrick's coat off a hook and hurried his boyfriend into it before his mom saw more than he wanted her to ever see.

"Where did you find those?" *Is he my boyfriend? Oh . . . I have a boyfriend?!*

"In a drawer." He shrugged. "I thought they were yours."

"Purple with stars? Do I look like a unicorn?"

"Now I see why you're cranky, even though you shouldn't be after hanky panky," his mom smirked knowingly.

Patrick's cheeks turned red, and Sandy couldn't help the foot stomp and sigh. "Stop. Please stop. And what is this?"

"It's for Patrick. Something from the auction."

"Actually, Annie, that's yours," Patrick replied.

Her features scrunched up and then a smile appeared. "But you bid on it."

"I did, but not for me, for your son."

The petite woman shook her head. "Show me what it is." She untied her boots as Sandy brought the box into the kitchen. He set it on the counter and grabbed his Xacto knife from a drawer.

"When did you have time to bid on anything?" Sandy said out of the corner of his mouth to Patrick.

"When you dashed off to save a stranger from a tree." Patrick helped open the box.

Together they extracted the portrait and laid it on the counter.

Mom stepped closer to get a better view of the photo. She clapped her hands over her mouth. "Oh no . . . you shouldn't have. This is too much."

"Your son told me he wanted to give this to you for Christmas, so . . . "

"She wasn't supposed to know that, and you're supposed to save money when you're jobless, not spend it." Sandy nudged Patrick with a shoulder.

Patrick gave Sandy a side squeeze. "It was for a good cause."

"I absolutely love it." She beamed at the photo and rested her head on Sandy's shoulder.

Sandy's heart sped up as he glanced between his mom and Patrick. He could get used to these feelings of love and warmth, and feeling that he was part of something bigger than himself. It was better than the scent of baked sugar cookies fresh out of the oven.

He couldn't deny it—this was the best feeling in the world.

ACKNOWLEDGMENTS

Late one evening during a writing sprint, my dearly departed friend, Colleen (aka Holly Ashby) said, "Sandy deserves a love story." She loved Sandy in Fast Love and she was adamant that Sandy find a partner. I will be forever grateful to Colleen for encouraging me to write Fast Holiday. While editing this book, I thought of her and hope that this novel would have met with her approval.

To the amazing, Chris Feldkamp, thank you for the love, conversations, and support. I'm uncertain who I would be without you in my life. You're my best friend (yes, I'll still be saying this when we're 100). You inspire me. Fast Holiday is for you. Many years ago, I promised to write you a story and I am nothing if not a woman of my word. It is with optimism that I know someday soon you will have a far superior love story than the fiction I have created. In the meantime, please enjoy this romp.

Thank you to the rockstar group of authors in Chapter HEA: Jacie Floyd, Julie Cameron, Raven Avellino, Holly Ashby, Delores Stewart, Janet Burnett, Cana Owens, Marcia Black, AG Sanders—all y'all brighten my life in ways I never expected. Thank you for your support, knowledge, encouragement, feedback, and beta reads on Fast Holiday. I would be lost without all y'all.

To my ridiculously talented artist, Steve Buccellato, thank you for your talent. You had the patience to read all of my emails, which I appreciate, and discuss my vision. The illustration and artwork of Sandy, Patrick, Moonshine, and Mayfield is absolutely perfect.

Jacie, the time and consideration that you put into your feedback is truly above and beyond. Thank you for your expertise, experience, guidance, and wisdom. I know mentoring me is an uphill battle. Thank you for taking on the challenge!

To my medical consultant, AG, thank you for allowing me to text you random questions about medical conditions.

Skye Malone, and Sara Whitney, thank you for being here and allowing me to ask y'all out-of-the-blue author questions.

Jorge, Michelle, Oren and Andrew Rodas, I love y'all so much. Thank you for the encouragement, support, and for the unconditional love.

Thanks Beck, Jack, Jack, John, Matt, Ruth, and William, for your support and love.

To my amazing, mom, thank you for listening to me rant and rave. You are my north compass. I love you.

ABOUT THE AUTHOR

Kerry Lockhart is a queer author with the heart of a wanderer. A Wisconsin ex-pat, she has lived in six different states in the USA. When she's not writing, she explores record stores, downhill skis, and discovers new hiking trails with her dog, Watson. She holds a master's degree in screenwriting and loves to revisit classic films, particularly those directed by Hitchcock or featuring Hepburn. To find out which Hepburn, follow Kerry at kerrylockhart.com.

Interested in learning more about Kerry and her books? Join her mailing list at https://kerrylockhart.com/news letter/

Visit Spotify to listen to the Fast Holiday playlist, https:// open.spotify.com/playlist/1p07B1vBGTTNKIb0vcFsqg?si= 7e99804b90724dba

instagram.com/kalwriter

goodreads.com/kerry_lockhart

amazon.com/stores/Kerry-Lockhart/author/B0C7D3F68Q

facebook.com/kerrylockhartauthor

x.com/kalwriter

EXCERPT FROM FAST LOVE

The Los Angeles Airport resembled a circus that featured fake boobs, toned bodies, and too many hipster hats. Julia detangled her glasses off the top of her head, catching a few brunette strands in the hinges before stuffing them into her bag. Characters of all sorts aimlessly wandered in and out of overpriced emporiums with their faces glued to their phones. Rarely did people make eye contact unrelated to a celebrity spotting. Why were there so many damn pretty people in the airport? Did they think they were auditioning for a movie? Or worse, reality TV?

Julia gripped the arm of her assistant, Sandy Holiday, as they made their way through the plethora of bodies. So much more than a writer's assistant, the Korean-American photographer had dropped into Julia's life at her first book signing. They'd formed an immediate bond over margaritas and their

disgust for Satan's playthings, the flip-flop. He'd soon gradu-
ated from part-time gofer to full-time confidant, psychoana-
lyst, enabler, and best friend.

They trudged along with Sandy, shouldering through
with his bag of camera equipment on his thick frame. He
stood a couple of inches taller than Julia, not entirely a difficult feat considering her five-foot-four height. He blew his
ebony bangs out of his eyes. "Okay, explain to me why you're
on the fence about your sister's wedding? Or does your
twitchiness have more to do with what's going on with Lady
McDeath and you?"

"It's fine. Everything is fine. It's this contract renegotiation
stuff, so our work and personal relationship are in a weird
place. Also, please stop calling my fiancée that name."

A stylish older woman with Chanel sunglasses and over-
arching eyebrows accompanied by a young man with a
ridiculous Greek god physique shot Julia a glare. The pair of
sour, judge-y faces that looked like they hadn't uttered the
word carbohydrate, much less smelled a carb in either of their
lifetimes, kept staring at them.

Frazzled and in a state of sensory overload, she couldn't
keep from shouting at the gawkers, "Go eat a bagel!"

Sandy clutched her elbow. "Have you gone completely
batshit cray cray?" He smirked at the couple. "Sorry. She
should be medicated, inebriated, or maybe put down."

The couple sped up and disappeared.

"That's one way to introduce yourself to the gorgeous
people of LA." Sandy stopped walking. "What's up?"

"Between the wedding, bickering with Nicole, my writer's

block, and my fledgling novel—what do you mean, *what's up*? Is it not *obvious*!?" Her hands flapped in the air, her entire body vibrating with nervous energy.

With his head sinking into his body, he smiled at a few people giving them the side-eye. "She's a queer historical romance author. This is perfectly normal," he assured them. Gently, he rested his hands on her shoulders. "We're making a stop." He took her bag, adding it to his other shoulder, then spun her around, steering her toward Molly Malone's Irish Pub.

"What about our bags? It's too early for cocktails."

"It's LA. I'm sure there'll be a delay long enough for you to chill the fuck out. Happy hour begins when the sun comes up."

There was nothing remotely Irish about the too-modern bar with its open concept, bright lights, and multiple big-screen televisions. The bar was full of day drinkers watching *SportsCenter*, eating pretzels, and enjoying overpriced drinks. Once they settled at the crowded bar, she had one shot of Bushmills down while he nursed his first appletini. The whiskey finally released the edge she teetered on. Her shoulders relaxed, dropping from her ears. Because of her diminutive size, the forty percent alcohol level hit her like a slap to the face. At this moment, being a cheap date had its advantages.

"All better?" He patted her arm.

Her head bounced up and down. She inhaled and released a breath. "All right. You know I visited PJ last—"

He made a rolling motion with his hand for her to get to the point as he sipped his drink.

She slid a bowl of pretzels out of reach. "My sister and Aiden wanted to take me someplace LA glamorous, so they dragged me to Sky Bar."

"You hate those types of places." He tore into the apple slice garnish, nibbling it with squirrel-like bites as he listened to her rant about her night out with her sister and her questionable fiancé.

———

Just before the onslaught of caffeine deprivation, Bobbi slid her tall frame into the only vacant space at the Irish-themed bar and flagged down the bartender to order coffee. An instant pang of regret hit her about throwing away her breakfast in anger after a message from her ex, Taylor. Neither the woman nor the gesture had been worth the waste of food. She scanned the lackluster bar menu and opted for a quick snack. When Bobbi reached across the bar to grab the bowl of pretzels, the person next to her shifted. As she turned, her breasts accidentally squished into the arm of the woman beside her.

"Excuse me?" The blue-eyed stunner shot Bobbi a raised eyebrow.

"Oh, you mind?" Bobbi held up a pretzel and stepped back, removing her chest with as much grace as she could muster.

The cheeks of the smaller woman blazed red. She cleared

her throat as she lifted her gaze from Bobbi's cleavage. "It's morning. Who eats pretzels this early?"

I might be low on caffeine, but I'm certain she checked me out. Bobbi glanced around. "Are you the pretzel police?" she whispered as the corners of her mouth lifted.

The bartender slid a coffee and sugar her way. Normally, Bobbi skipped sugar, but since surviving the small commuter plane ride, which rattled like her first stock car—held together with glue and duct tape—she indulged. Her gaze traveled to the feisty brunette sitting next to her in a pair of ripped-knee jeans. Smooth peach skin peeked through the shredded gap, flawless except for a vertical scar on the left knee. The small imperfection tugged at her heart. She had plenty of injuries herself from accidents over the years. Bobbi had a hunch a good story was behind that mark.

"Or are you busting me for eating a snack food?" she asked, somehow compelled to interact with this intriguing stranger. Maybe even get under her skin a bit. "That's not ginger ale in your shot glass."

"Wrong. I always drink ginger ale . . . in very tiny doses."

"Sure, you do." Bobbi let the corner of her mouth rise in a taunt.

The brunette squinted at her and then turned back to her fuzzy-armed friend while Bobbi openly eavesdropped. "Anyway, I went to the restroom, and when I made my way back to the table, I noticed him at the bar. He wasn't alone."

"Not your sister?" Fuzzy Arms sipped and puckered his lips as the brunette shook her head.

"Could have been a friend." While blowing on the steaming cup of coffee, Bobbi dropped in the comment.

"Hello? Private conversation." With eyes flashing, the pocket-sized beauty shifted her hands back and forth between herself and her friend.

"Or a co-worker?" She couldn't resist. The brunette's cute, angry-puppy energy drew her in. The pink of her cheeks had deepened the more they bantered, and Bobbi wanted to see if she could coerce that blush further into the V of her button-down.

"M'kay, that's possible, Jules," Fuzzy Arms agreed.

"For your inquisitive mind, the bartender informed me that the woman in question was of ill repute."

Delighted by the word choice, the corners of Bobbi's mouth twitched. "Ill repute? Did we time-travel to the 1800s? Where's the TARDIS parked?"

The woman, referred to as 'Jules' tossed back her shot, followed by a scoff.

"Has someone watched *Pretty Woman* one too many times?" Bobbi's shoulders shook as she held in her laughter.

The brunette drummed her fingers across the bar. "Are you saying I'm the type of woman to sit around filing my nails, streaming rom-coms, and reading romance novels on my Kindle?"

Trying not to be too obvious, Bobbi leaned in closer to the blue-eyed knockout. The woman's tantalizing citrusy scent made everything go blurry. "Now that was overly detailed." Her voice dipped with studied intimacy.

Jules' mouth gaped open and then closed.

"But now I'm curious . . . what do you do for a living?"

She blinked as if trying to clear her thoughts. "I'm . . . I write. I'm a writer."

"And you write what? Romance novels?"

The loud gasp from the diminutive beauty turned a few heads at the bar. "What? How? What?!" She looked at her friend to save her from the conversation, but his nose had taken up residence in his phone.

"I can't believe I got it in one guess. What are the odds?" Bobbi gloated. Ever since entering the motorsports limelight, she never picked up women. They came to her sometimes looking for sex and other times, money. It was hard to trust their motives, but there was something about the energy between her and the shorter woman that made this exchange fun and free of strings. *Probably because she doesn't know who I am. Shit, that sounded like my dad.*

"And what do you do, Ms. All Important Big Shot?"

Bobbi shifted in her chair and opened her blazer, revealing a GK Racing tank top. "I'm the only Japanese-American woman driver on the stock car circuit. You don't watch sports, do you?" Bobbi followed the brunette's gaze down to the amount of cleavage she had on display. *Ha, yeah, you're busted, Brontë. She's not suddenly impressed by your career? That's refreshing.*

"Who has the time to stream anything? And, heh, that figures," Jules said.

Fuzzy Arms grasped his friend's elbow. "Okay, I'm back. So, did you ever find out who the mystery woman was?"

She relaxed her posture, returning to their original conversation. "I don't know for certain if she was with him, *with* him, but—"

"Jumping to conclusions is always a good idea." Bobbi stood up, shooting Jules a sultry smirk while leaning on an elbow on the bar. "Also, what does *that figures* imply?"

"Oh, I think you know . . . driving around in circles all day. I mean, I doubt you had to spend a lot of time studying for that kind of career." The brunette threw the words over her shoulder and then busied her hands by toying with the buttons on her shirt.

Bobbi caught the nervous gesture. *Did she really believe that?* "Hey, maybe your sister's boyfriend was giving her directions?" she suggested, reluctant to walk away.

"To what? His fly?"

The deep bubble of laughter from Bobbi surprised them all. This adorable creature's wit moved faster than Bill Elliott's Ford Thunderbird.

Fuzzy Arms glanced back and forth between them. "You two are *hilarious*."

"And another thing," Bobbi said, tossing a few bills on the bar, "just because I drive in circles doesn't mean I'm one-dimensional. I'd think a writer would recognize that. Unless—"

"What? *Unless* what?"

Bobbi rested a hand on the back of the other woman's chair. She leaned in close to her ear. "Unless you're not all that imaginative. Maybe you need a long, hard session with a muse to inspire you?" Bobbi whirled around and walked away, sporting a giant grin.

————

Julia had a comeback on the tip of her tongue. A good one too. As she stood to follow, she caught her foot on the rung of the bar stool and took a nosedive to the ground.

Sandy steepled his fingers together as he peered down at her. "Coffee?"

The groan she released came from her bruised pride and not the impact of the floor. "Iced, please." The heat of the whiskey had hit her at exactly the wrong moment. She could blame her tumble on the alcohol, right? Or maybe someone fudged the thermostat? Who the hell was that incredibly striking, yet maddening woman?

The bartender and waiter took pity on them, helping Julia up and handing her an iced coffee and a bag of crushed ice, probably praying she wouldn't sue them for a faulty bar stool. As they walked away from the embarrassing scene, she held the cold compress against the lump on her forehead. "Here, hold this." They stopped moving, so she could drop the ice and her coffee in Sandy's palms as she dug her glasses and pen out of a zipper pocket in her bag. "How is it I have nothing to write on?"

As the lightning bolt of inspiration struck, she had to get notes on paper, any kind of paper, before it evaporated into the ether of lost ideas. From her pants pocket, she pulled several cocktail napkins. She slipped the glasses on her nose, writing furiously on the delicate tissue. She thought about the infuriating woman from the bar.

She was unnerved by how quickly the woman had

affected her and slipped past her defenses. What was worse, she couldn't stop thinking about her auburn eyes, seducing her with a wily twinkle when she smiled. The memory of her long legs and the tight tank especially remained lodged front and center in her mind, something that she likely wouldn't forget for a long time.

"So . . . she was sexy."

Her brow furrowed. "Huh?"

"Oh, please, sweetie, I may not speak the language of Lesbos, but even Robert Bunsen would agree there was something a brewin' between you two."

"Bunsen?"

"Famous chemist, who also had invented flash photography?" He looked at her like the entire world could have grasped that obvious connection.

"Winner of most obscure reference. Ding, ding, ding!"

He tapped his foot in an almost irritating manner. "You're deflecting."

"She was fine. Nothing stellar," she lied, training her eyes on the revolving baggage. He'd see through her fib in a hot second. "Need I remind you, I'm an engaged woman."

He did an obnoxious snort-laugh. "Nothing lasts forever, sweet cheeks. Speaking of your betrothed, when do you plan on announcing that you're thinking of dumping her as your agent? When you're standing in front of the pastor? Minister? Genie? Did you land on an officiant?"

She shrugged and gestured for him to move along. "Pass."

"What do you think this is? A game show?"

"You'd be the hostess with the mostest." She tucked the napkin into her bag.

"Mmm hmm." He pulled his luggage off the carousel.

"Soon, all right? I'll tell her soon. Although, I can't tell her on the phone, and I'm certainly not going to text her that news. A DM would be rude."

"Before or after the honeymoon?"

"What about during? She'd be more relaxed."

Inserting his rolling duffle between them, he smirked. "You mean inebriated."

The honeymoon was another sticking point. Julia wanted to relax someplace like the mountains or the beach. Or even Europe. However, her fiancée insisted on a typeface tour and workshop. While she agreed fonts were interesting in a dry-wheat toast kind of way, they weren't something she wanted to spend countless hours learning about, especially during a romantic getaway.

"What difference does it make what agency I'm with in the long run?" she said.

"Absolutely none to me. But it makes a helluva lot of difference to Lady McDeath." He folded his arms across his chest. "Out of curiosity, does she know anything about you?" His usual flip expression creased into concern.

Warning! Bad sign. Anxiety crawled its way across her shoulders like the spidery innkeeper's hands from her third novel. She didn't have time for these worries. After all, they had a wedding to attend. Unfortunately, she'd be dealing with her mother, too.

"Sure. Yeah. Yes." Her stomach churned with unease. A

small bubble of acid reflux rose from her stomach up to her throat. "Of course." She caught her reflection in a darkened monitor where her disbelieving eyes stared back at her. Ugh. The lies. The burning in a fiery pit from all the lies. She'd always wondered about the exact temperature in Hell. Turns out it was approximately the same as Los Angeles. "We're going to need a bigger bottle of sunscreen . . . and a triple pack of Tums." She spotted her luggage rounding the corner.

She hustled to the reclaim area and struggled to yank her gear free. As the luggage traveled, she practically jogged with it and pulled and jogged and pulled on it some more. Out of the corner of her eye, she spotted the race car driver, amused at her struggles. Julia noticed the woman stepping closer. She was certain the driver was going to offer her services as if Julia were some damsel in distress. She used all her strength and gave the damn thing a last tug. It broke free, whirling Julia around in a circle, and smacked the driver square in the shoulder, sending her flying onto the bags and carousel. The driver groaned out an *oof* on impact.

"Better luck next time, Stretch!" Julia snickered as she scooted away. Her heart rate picked up. *Am I fearful that the long-legged woman might chase me down or afraid she won't?*

EXCERPT FROM FAST LOVE
CHAPTER 2

Despite the dry heat, the serenity of The Vanderbell Club's yoga veranda with the birds-of-paradise and the draping bougainvillea almost guaranteed Bobbi a good day. The space didn't have any late morning classes, so she had the area to herself. And the clever location allowed only the sounds of nature instead of club noise. Bobbi set her things on a railing before rolling out her personal mat.

Favoring her left arm from last night's crash and the right from today's luggage encounter, she stretched into a half-moon pose through a string of curse words. The light crept through the open-air gallery, soothing her with the warm rays. She hummed, relishing the cool breeze from a ceiling fan that tickled her skin through her muscle shirt. Grateful for the liberty to stretch without having to apologize for her long limbs and popping joints to her body-obsessed former lover.

Sure, Taylor's blonde windswept hair and dazzling smile, in contrast to Bobbi's sweaty face and racing jumpsuit, made them look like the perfect couple in photos. In motorsports, keeping up appearances came in second only to winning.

She couldn't explain why the spitfire from the airport popped into her head at that precise moment. That move she'd pulled at baggage should have pissed Bobbi off. Instead, it had the opposite effect. *Why didn't I get her number?* Even though Bobbi and her ex broke up months ago, her bumpy past relationship still messed with her confidence— no surprise her head wasn't on the track the other night.

She balanced on one leg and slipped into a warrior pose and then switched to the other leg. A groan slipped out when a reminder displayed on her iWatch. Guy the Car Guy's Motorsports podcast interview loomed overhead like a menacing thundercloud. A half-hour of power yoga had refreshed her, which she needed for the call with Guy. She blotted her face and ears with a towel, then collected her earbuds, phone, and iPad from the railing. As she slipped the buds into her ears, her watch and iPad buzzed. *He had to be on time, didn't he?*

"How's that sassy Bobbi doin' this bright and beautiful day?" He had that used car salesman voice, which grated on her last nerve. He sounded cheerful, as if he was about to screw someone out of a fortune.

"Never better, Guy." She plastered a fake smile on her face to prepare herself for the rough ride ahead.

"Great, great. Stay with me. We go live in 10 seconds. Ready to roll?"

"Fire away." To make the time with him less painful, she popped one of her ear buds out of her ear and lowered the volume on her iPad. She swore the audience could hear him in all time zones from his intense decibels.

"Hello race fans. Welcome! I'm Guy the Car Guy. This morning we're sitting pretty and have the hot-to-trot Bobbi Yoshida-Barnes, driver of car number 37, with us. Tough break on last night's race. Didn't see that blowout comin', am I right?" His chuckle oozed with fake sympathy.

She released a breath, refusing to laugh with him at her own expense. Although Amy, her media representative, would tell her to play along and then say something about honey and flies. Unfortunately, her shoulder flared up, not to be inconspicuous, she rolled it, hoping he wouldn't notice her wince. *Focus on the question.* She'd known he'd ask this question. But did it have to be the first question instead of the last? *Be brief. Be concise. Stay focused.* "Unfortunately, we did not."

"Come on, that's all we're getting out of you?"

She pulled out a vague answer from her Media 101 tool kit. "We learn from our mistakes as much as our wins. The takeaway is how we use the knowledge during the next race."

"Do you think it's difficult being a part of a male-dominated sport?"

"Not any more so than being a woman working in any industry." She bit back what she really wanted to say, which was that the homophobia and crap she had to endure as a lesbian, Asian, female racer far outweighed what the guys could ever handle.

But Bobbi knew that was exactly the kind of sound bite that Guy drooled over. She would never complain. No matter how rough her road was—she rose above and would stick it to them all on the track. Plus, she supported the Drive to Equality Program to ensure that the future of her sport changed for the better.

A chime sounded from her iPhone. She glanced at the device and saw Mack, her crew chief, beaming in from his office at the track. Obviously, he'd tuned in to the podcast and thought she needed moral support. She hit the green FaceTime button and pumped the volume down so only she could hear.

"There have been some amazing women drivers in stock car racing." Offscreen from the podcast, she wagged a hand at Mack.

He raised an eyebrow as a greeting, knowing not to say much during the live interview. Even on a small screen, his stocky body made him look like Winnie the Pooh stuck in a honey pot. A headphone dangled from one of his ears with the other end tucked into his shirt collar.

"It was probably more challenging being Ethel Mobley in the 40s or Janet Guthrie in the 70s versus today. Doesn't matter if the person in my rearview is a man or woman; it only means that I'm in the lead. Which is where I prefer to be all the time."

Guy issued his smarmy chuckle again. "You get the Barnes spirit from your daddy. What challenges do you find being a lesbian in stock car racing?"

"Fucking little prick," Mack grumbled.

"Is that pretty girlfriend of yours with you or still in bed? What do you two sleep in?"

Was he serious? The ass. She tilted her head back. *Damn bees and honey!* "No matter what pj's I favor, being a lesbian makes me good with my hands and able to shift quicker." She rolled her eyes at Mack, who snickered at the sarcastic reply.

That got a raucous laugh out of Guy, but Bobbi continued.

"She's not here. You'd have to check with her about her pajamas since I don't know anymore."

"Uh-oh, sounds like there's trouble in paradise!"

The prerecorded sound of a cat screaming played.

For a brief second, she slipped off camera exchanging grimaces with Mack at the absurdity of Guy's antics.

"Someone should knock him in the nutsack." Mack massaged his ear.

She blew out a slow breath, trying to keep her laughter inside. "We broke up and the dissolution was amicable."

"That's a scoop y'all heard first on Guy the Car Guy's Show. All right, we're going to take a quick break. When we return, we'll talk next-gen cars and tech . . ."

The interview ended an hour later, and Bobbi dropped her head as soon as she was off the call.

"Guy's a moron." Mack popped the headphone out of his ear and wrapped the cord around his phone.

"Everything he said sounded salacious."

"No shit. That's why he's got an audience." Hunched over his desk, he slathered butter on a piece of toast. "You all right?"

She leaned on the railing, thinking about how simply

everything came together in the beginning, before the press, before increased requests for interviews. "Our go-kart racing and street cars days were way easier."

Mack snorted, his way of agreeing with her. The one reliable face in the ever-revolving door of her life on and off the track belonged to Mack. Taller than her in the early days, she towered over him now with her five-foot-nine frame. She teased him it was because after he turned fifty-five, all that coffee he drank finally stunted his growth.

She unscrewed the cap on her water bottle. A voicemail message from Taylor flashed on her phone. "Nope, not today, Goblin." She gulped down some water.

"How's the elbow holding up, Kid?"

She flexed her arm back and forth. "Still bends." Opening a protein bar presented an especially fun challenge with her arm stiff from last night's blowout on the track.

"By the by, Kit says better luck next time."

Thankfully, her boss and the owner of GK Racing's off-the-cuff message meant she still had a job. The blowout hadn't seemed bad, but when the car spun out on the lawn, she slammed against the side, smashing her left arm between her body and the door. Her shoulder hurt like someone had whacked it with a baseball bat. An ugly bruise and a scratch decorated her elbow. Trying not to dwell on the accident only made it ache worse. She replayed it over in her head on an endless loop.

Could she have reacted differently? Maybe make an earlier pit stop to have the tires swapped out? She knew she could have eased back on the accelerator on the oil-slicked pavement; instead, she pushed the machine harder. Sick of placing in the double digits, yesterday's reckless performance revealed her desperate desire to win. Kit might have been understanding, but there would be a price to pay with her sponsor and of that she was certain.

Mack bit into his toast, then abruptly stopped chewing. She followed his gaze behind her. An all-too familiar couple walked down the stairs.

Mack grunted. "Heard Dick's on a rampage."

"What's new?" Although she'd finally opened the wrapper, her appetite had vanished with this unannounced appearance. It was a thing he did, the tyrant, showing up out of the blue, to throw people off. Unfortunately, the tactic worked like a charm on her, and this morning his presence only added more stress to her unbalanced world.

"Heh. Yeah." Mack took a sip from his coffee mug. "That tire blowing out last night—"

"NBCS has it on a loop along with some old accident footage. Caught it last night on TikTok with EDM underneath it . . . *EDM*," she muttered the acronym like it embodied the worst possible insult.

"Ah, shit, Kid, no one likes EDM." Mack dug a finger into his ear. "What's EDM?"

She shook her head as she laughed at his musical genre foibles. "I guess the next thing I can look forward to is some kind of TMZ smash up of my love life on the internet."

Taking a moment to shift in his chair, the grizzled crew chief avoided eye contact. "She gone for good?" He stuffed the rest of the toast in his mouth. "I never liked her. Always smelled like hair dye," he said as a couple of crumbles flew at his screen.

The corners of her lips twitched as she held back her amusement. "Hair dye?"

"Yeah, ya know, plastic." He winked.

She could always count on him for his humor. Out of the corner of her eye, she caught him rubbing the back of his neck. There was something on his mind, and if there was one thing she knew, it was that Mack wouldn't bring today's topic up until she forced his hand. "Out with it." She breathed out a heavy, dread-filled sigh.

"The rumor true . . . She seein' someone on the side?"

She shrugged, disinterested in deconstructing the relationship. Taylor wasn't her problem anymore. Surprised he paid any attention to gossip, she thought about saying so, but changed her mind. It didn't matter. "What do you think?"

"I think you wouldn't have kicked her to the curb if it weren't."

"That and about a million other things was how she landed on the concrete, my friend." She picked at the edges of the protein bar as her eyes traveled to her two visitors.

"Is old Dick stopping by to give us a pep talk?" Mack's shoulders shook with a chuckle.

"We'll be lucky if he lets us buy a new set of tires," Bobbi said.

A pointy-nosed redhead stepped up to the veranda, followed by Bobbi's sponsor.

They were in close enough range that Mack could see and hear them clearly through his screen. Her crew chief nodded at the woman walking in step with Richard. "Think Red gets paid more than me?"

With a flat gaze in Mack's direction, Richard handed his cell to his assistant. "Mack."

"Dick."

Bobbi tucked the uneaten protein bar aside. She could practically hear the score to Jaws playing as she and her fearsome sponsor stared one another down. Their war had been a battle that had gone on for far too long. She imagined that it'd last until one or both were six feet underground.

"Better go see if my assistant to my assistant's ass has any messages for me." The crew chief downed his coffee and slammed the empty cup on his desk.

"Later." Bobbi threw a nod in his direction.

"Yeah, Kid." Mack saluted, and the screen went dark.

"We need to have a conversation." Richard folded his arms over his puffed-up chest. Six feet tall and fit, when the man chose to intimidate, that one change to his posture worked like gangbusters. She'd seen it a million times, and by now, she found his posturing annoying.

"It was a blowout. The pit can't predict—"

"If you had a better crew chief, you could. He should have called you in two laps prior—"

She flipped her iPad cover shut, avoiding his steely gaze. *To hell with him if I'll admit anything.* "That was my call. Mack can't force me into the pit."

"I think you wanted that accident to happen."

"Hold on." She held up a hand to get him to slow down.

Richard slammed a fist into the palm of his other hand. "Ever since the Daytona crash—"

"That was at the beginning of the year."

"Your performance has gone downhill and the man that should get you back to standards, hell, beyond that, is coddling you," he argued.

She rocked back on her heels. "What are we talking about here?" She compared the sinking sensation in her stomach to a tire deflating. His tone seemed to lead up to something and that something, she'd bet, defined abysmal.

His phone beeped, but his assistant picked it up. Turning, the robotic female walked a couple of steps away, out of earshot of the imminent argument.

"Either fire Mack or find yourself new sponsors." With that pronouncement, Richard stormed away. He snatched the phone from his assistant and then turned to face Bobbi, holding the device to his chest. "Your brother's meet and greet for the wedding is this afternoon. Don't be late." A Town Car rolled across the grounds toward them.

"Hey, I'm the one that always shows up for him. Remind me, what was the make and model of Aiden's first car?" She stared him down, refusing to blink in their competition.

His face and neck turned pink enough that the artery in his neck throbbed visibly.

Patiently, she waited him out, knowing she'd win any argument regarding Aiden. As his older sister, she'd designated herself a protector from all things labeled Dad Bullshit.

"Nineteen ninety-nine, Toyota Tercel, used two-door, red. Bought it all on his own. I taught him how to change the oil.

Since you have done nothing for him, I'm curious why you'd give a shit about his wedding?"

A ripple of joy traveled through her veins as her father stormed off. And seeing him enter the Town Car without the aid of his chauffeur, then slamming the door made one upping him in a petty argument feel like a podium finish.

Regrettably, the elation crashed. She picked up her cell phone and paced back and forth. She wanted to call Mack but hated the idea of filling him in on Richard's ultimatum. He'd probably get pissed, tell her dad to shove the job up his ass, and quit in a huff. "Damn it," she grumbled to the device.

She stopped pacing. Taylor's voicemail stared at her. It might be avoidance of the real problem, but today verged on a cruddy day, so why not embrace a full-blown cruddy day with the voice of *El Diablo* included? She couldn't resist the temptation. She hit play.

"Listen, I'm picking up the last of my stuff today. You better not be there. And I'm keeping Moonshine. I watered her, fed her, and had her spayed."

Bobbi threw her phone across the veranda with a screech. Losing her dog was the proverbial cherry on the shit sundae.